THE END RAIDERS

THE END RAIDERS

EVELYN C. CAMPBELL

To
the edelweiss
For letting me borrow
its beautiful name

One

My mind flutters around, searching for something. Anything. Anything to prove my father's worth. A memory. An item. His words. What has he given me? Why does he deserve the title of Father?

The cause of my unrest is in the kitchen with my mother. He is older than I had imagined, with silver streaks in his dark hair and beard. The ugly scar below his left cheek proves he has been in battle. He must be brave, leaving his family to fight against the End Raiders. He is one of the rarities who do, for almost everyone nowadays fully supports the End Raider empire. I am one of the only people who don't care. Even the schoolgirls hold an interest in politics. Not me. I'm not a politician.

But it's not just politics that outcasts me from my peers. After all, the girls are far more concerned about their future husbands. All the town girls have their choice in Seth Sound's finest men. Not me. I'm stuck. I'm the daughter of a poverty-stricken villager, so I have to marry the rare town boy who goes for poor girls like me. My father arranged my marriage with a boy who works at his family repair shop. He invites me to his house almost daily, but we both know he does it only for his parents.

Among my fiancé's faults is his name. *Vashti.* What were his parents thinking, giving him a girl's name? Besides, he may live in the town with the wealthier folk, but he's still lower-class. He might scrape by to make a living for himself and me, but it won't be a comfortable life.

I'm sitting on my parent's bed and staring at the floor. Enough of that. I have more to worry about than Vashti. My father is the current threat.

Years ago, when I was eight, my father left to fight in the War of the Raiders. At first, I was proud to be his daughter, but then I realized no one approved when I told them so. They either looked sympathetic, angry, embarrassed, or mocking. I hate that. I hate it when they laugh at my father, at me, because to them, he is fighting on the wrong side.

"Edelweiss," trills my mother, who has been positively loopy since my father returned. She is under the impression that, with him back, our family will be okay and have money again. I'm not silly enough to believe that. Our family broke beyond repair the day my father left.

"Edelweiss, where are you? Come and see your father. You haven't left your bedroom since we came home."

I obediently walk in, sit at the tiny kitchen table, and heave a sigh. My father frowns.

"Good to see you, Ed," he greets me, though his expression says the opposite.

The name Ed stirs my memory. Nobody ever calls me Ed except my father. Once he left eight years ago, I forgot about it.

"How are you?" he continues.

"I'm fine," I say with a shrug.

"Is that all you have to say for years of separation?"

"It hasn't been too exciting around here, though most men go away for a shorter vacation." My father opens his mouth in protest but closes it again, so my mother intervenes.

"Your father has been through a lot. Please have a little compassion, Edelweiss."

"I would, if only he were fighting on the right side."

"Now, wait a moment," he rebukes. My father never fails to become passionate when the End Raiders are praised. "The End Raiders' reign over the Realm was the most corrupt 200 years of human existence."

"Your father has had to juggle providing for his political beliefs and his family, Edelweiss." My mother pats his hand.

"Is that so, Mother? Then why do I feel like you and I have been fending for ourselves over these past eight years?"

"Let's have a little appreciation for your father's sacrifices."

"It's not a lack of appreciation, Mother; it's a lack of tolerance." With that, I push back my chair and go outside.

I walk to town, thinking about my father and the End Raiders. What is so horrible about a central government? Everyone in Seth Sound supports it. Seth Sound's king, Roe, is the leader of the empire.

I enter town and head for Mr Greene's bank, where I count my slim earnings and deposit the funds. There I see my only friend.

"Edelweiss!" calls Mr Greene, chuckling. He has silver hair and an English mustache. He is always bubbly and bouncy; I don't believe I have ever seen him in a bad mood.

"Hello, sir," I say dryly. I'm surprised at how mild I sound- usually, I'm full of emotion.

"What can I do for you, my dear?" He beams, like always, without a particular reason.

"Oh, nothing," I say, wishing I had an excuse for my visit. "Just... um... I wanted to know how much money is in my mother's account."

"Oh yes, of course," Mr Greene agrees and whisks away to find out. My father had left some money in his bank account, meant to last my mother and me a few months- but he ended up being gone for much longer. My mother and I had started our own fund to deposit earnings in, but we are often without work.

Mr Greene returns, smiling. He's about to answer my inquiry when a family steps through the door. Mr Greene is easily distracted as he forgets I'm still there. I am about to walk out the door when I notice who the family is- the Kinlings.

The head of the Kinling family is John K. Everyone calls him that, even his wife. He makes a ton of money owning a casino, and I'm sure he would never leave his family to fight a losing war. His wife is a snobby lady named Martha Kinling.

They have two children, Lizzie and Thomas. Lizzie has long, blonde locks and wears pretty dresses. Adults all think she's an angel. She is my age and was in my class when I was still in school. Her little brother, Thomas, is a temperamental troublemaker. People think he's cute because he's timid around grown-ups, but it's all a pretense. Thomas is mischievous and shuns poor children. The second I see the Kinlings, I wish I had never come to the bank. I begin walking to the exit when Mrs Kinling stops me.

"Wait, girl. What's your name again? Never mind. You're a Chapel, though, I know that. Your father just came home, didn't he? The soldier who fights against the End Raiders? So ignorant... Say, you *are* engaged, aren't you?" she rambles. My cheeks burn. I hate talking about my fiance, especially with Mrs Kinling.

"Yes, ma'am," I say evenly, conscious of my tone. "I will soon marry Vashti Marlow. He lives in town." Mrs Kinling stares at me blankly.

"Marlow, eh? I'm not sure I'm familiar with a Marlow. He must not have much class, or I might... well..." She begins to mumble to herself, so I slip out the door with a quick wave to Lizzie. Mrs Kinling is right. Vashti Marlow does live in town, but he's nothing special. He works at his family's repair shop.

If only he were rich! If only I could have fancy dresses, go to elaborate balls, and eat elegant food. I would have everything I could ever want. People would envy me for a change, and I would have friends who are my equals.

I kick myself mentally. I cannot afford to think like that. Soon, I will be Mrs Vashti Marlow, a poor man's wife. We will both work long hours for the rest of our lives, struggling to keep the repair shop afloat. We will not retire and probably die young. Our children, if we have any, will carry on our legacy in poverty, and that will be it. No miracle will save me, nothing to make anything different. This is the truth, and I must accept it. But why is it so hard?

Two

When I wake up the following day, the sky is torched in a dusky purple haze. My parents are still asleep, their arms wrapped around each other. I shake my head in disbelief. Those eight years seem to mean nothing to my mother. She has been a desperate, single mother for so long, striving to stay afloat, working tirelessly, even going without eating. Now my father is back, but she acts as if nothing is his fault, as if he has not abandoned her.

I stagger outside and jog in the opposite direction of the town. Though sleepy, I find the best time to do this errand is in the morning. I'm heading to the berry patch, where I can pick berries and do my thinking. Sometimes, town folk or villagers outside of town will come here, looking for something to make pies out of, but I come just to sit, think, and gorge myself on the small fruits.

I am eating tiny red strawberries when I hear someone approaching. I had hoped to be the only one here this morning, but it's not unusual for someone else to join me. Only, I do not expect this person, of all people, to turn up.

I don't look to verify who it is because I can tell that it is Vashti by his whistling.

"Hey," he greets me. I glance at him and then back at the strawberry in my fingers.

"Vashti." I have lost all my appetite for berries, though he looks like a starved man as he wolfs down five, ten, fifteen strawberries.

After he has eaten his fill, he swallows and addresses me. "I haven't seen you in a while. Where have you been lately?" I have indeed avoided him recently. Usually, my mother pressures me to spend time with him, but with my father coming home, she's given up on that.

"I've been busy," I mutter. Vashti suddenly brightens up.

"Oh yeah," he says. "Your father came back from the war, didn't he?"

"That's right," I reply. "He's been serving for eight years." Vashti seems impressed by this.

"Your father's on the right side, you know," he admits. "I don't usually make this public, but I don't like the End Raiders so much. They scare me. Too controlling, I guess." I didn't even consider which side of the war Vashti is on. I guess this is why my father wants me to marry him.

"My father would be happy to hear you say that," I respond, not knowing anything about politics.

"So," he says, and I'm relieved to get off the End Raider subject. "You want to come to my house after this?" I hesitate before replying because as much as I despise the possibility of marrying Vashti, I *will* marry him, and it will do no good to be hostile about it. I should start seeing him again and get used to his company, but I can't bring myself to act off this right now.

"I can't. My mother is doing her summer cleaning, and I'm supposed to help her," I lie.

"Oh," Vashti says, and he seems genuinely disappointed, which confuses me. "Do you want me to help you?"

"No." The last thing I need is for Vashti to discover the untruth.

"Okay," he says. "I guess I should go then. You *will* stop by the repair shop sometime, won't you?"

"If I have anything to repair," I reply indifferently, just before taking the cue. "Oh, I see. Yes, maybe I will stop by. Are you always there?" Vashti considers this for a second.

"I'll be there if I know you're coming."

"I'll be by tomorrow afternoon," I say guiltily. I have already turned him down twice today.

"Perfect," he says. "I look forward to it." He smiles and leaves me alone. I sit there numbly for a second longer before returning to my house. When I push open the door, I see that my parents are awake.

"Good morning," my mother sings as I walk in. It's not unusual for me to leave before she's awake. My father sips his black coffee and doesn't say a word, so I follow his lead and ignore him.

"Brought us some berries," I say, holding out a fistful I had pocketed before Vashti interrupted me.

"Oh, lovely," she says, stashing them away. "Eat some breakfast, Edelweiss." She hands me a plate of potatoes and bread. I eat in silence, and my parents communicate with their eyes. They seem to be trying to decide something. Once I have put the last potato in my mouth, my mother pounces.

"Edelweiss, we need to talk." I have no choice but to listen through my dread. "Vashti's parents agree that your marriage should be sooner rather than later. The date we have in mind is September the first."

"That's soon," is all I can choke out because my mouth rapidly dries up. That is less than two months to prepare! One thought occupies me: *I don't want to marry Vashti.* My parents will say he's a hard worker and will make money running the repair shop until their tongues stiffen, but I don't believe it. I will have to struggle to keep us alive, and we will never have time to enjoy life. If ever we have kids, it will make things worse for both them and us. Then there is the simple truth that I don't love Vashti. I hold back tears and stare at the floor.

"I know it's a quick transition, so I want you to ease into your new life by getting a job," my mother says gently. The ground swims before my eyes as I wipe away a rebellious tear.

"Fine," I hear myself croak, and I stand to leave.

"Edelweiss," my father calls, speaking for the first time. "Find a job soon. Then you can save up for something nice."

"That's ridiculous," I scoff. If I get any money, I will put every penny into the bank. Nothing nice will come of a job except survival later on.

Before my father can reply, I dash into the bedroom and sob into the mat that I now sleep on. While my father was away, I slept on the bed with my mother. Now, a mat suffices until I am married. No one disturbs me for an hour until my father enters the bedroom. He crouches down and puts a hand on my shoulder, but I slap it away at once. He sighs, and I hear him leave the house.

Once I feel I can't possibly cry another drop, I gather my wits and think. What job can I get? I am going through a long list of occupations in my mind when my mother bursts into the room. She seems to have forgotten how upset I am.

"Edelweiss!" she cries. "I found a job for you. Do you remember Miss Golden?" Yes, I remember Miss Golden. She had been my teacher since I was a young child, but I had dropped out since school is only free until you're fourteen. Only the richer kids go to school after they turn fourteen years old, and the classes are small. I haven't seen Miss Golden in two years.

"Well, the school has grown so much that Miss Golden is splitting it into two classes. You will teach the younger students, and she will teach the older ones." Fourteen years is a significant turning point in education, so it makes sense that Miss Golden won't have me teach the kids paying for school. I figure a job with my former teacher is the best I can ask for, so I accept her offer.

"Good girl!" my mother laughs. "Oh, and one other thing, Edelweiss." Her voice suddenly becomes stern. "Do be kind to Vashti. After all, he will soon be your husband."

"Yeah, I know. I'll try," I say, even though I'm sure I won't be good at it. If only Vashti would just put an end to this. If only he would fall in love with another girl and call off the marriage. *But then what?* I think. I should be grateful to Vashti. He's saving me from the terrible fate of living unmarried. In Seth Sound, no unmarried woman lives happily. A life with Vashti *must* be better than its alternative.

I wear my nicest clothes this morning: a white smock and, over it, a puffy blue dress. I tie a white ribbon to my curly brown hair.

I walk off the dirt road and in the grass so the dust doesn't kick up on my new black shoes. When I get to the schoolhouse, which is a long walk, class is about to begin.

Most boys are playing a game with a ball. The little girls are playing a chanting game called "Bubblegum" with their dainty feet. They all admire each girl's fancy shoes and tiny white socks while chanting a rhyme about bubblegum. Some older girls are reading books, while others chat with each other.

I see Lizzie Kinling among the talkative ones. Her golden locks are tied in ponytails with two rose-colored ribbons on the ends, draping down her front. She wears an expensive red dress. The Kinlings have got to be the wealthiest folk in town, though I'm sure their wealth doesn't hold a candle to what the government families have.

I stride inside the schoolhouse and find Miss Golden. When I do, she sits at her desk, smiling at me.

"Hello, Edelweiss; it's so good to see you again." I have always been one of her best students, so she was grieved when I had to drop out.

"Thank you, Miss Golden, for allowing me to return."

"It's my pleasure, dear. I do have an assignment for you. I need you to teach the little ones; you've seen me do it before. Call each class to your desk and use the guidebook to help you assign lessons, give tests, and run the school."

This sounds easy enough. She gives me a giant stack of books, each labeled *Guidebook*, but for a different subject or grade level. Miss Golden tells me that each student is at a different place in their curriculum, and I should mark each of them where they're at on Fridays so they'll have their places on Mondays.

I am right in that my duties are simple. Every day, I go from home to school and from school to home. The days at school go by quickly. Soon, however, it's the weekend, and I have to deal with my father, though we mostly steer clear of each other. The real trouble is Vashti, who constantly insists on us being together.

I will admit he is taking our situation better than I am. When I do consent to be in Vashti's company, he calls on me more often, and soon I see him every day, as he walks me home from school and spends all of the weekend with me. I see so much of Vashti that he's all I ever have time to think about.

One Friday, sick of him walking me home from school, I bravely tell him,

"Let's not see each other tomorrow. I have a lot to do." There's a long, awkward silence as he absorbs this.

"Okay," Vashti agrees, but he sounds rather hurt. "I love you." His abrupt words surprise me, which is ironic because he sees me daily, and we're engaged. I don't know what to say, so I just nod. As I turn to go inside my house, his voice stops me. "Do you love me?" I suck in my breath, but why lie to him? He'll soon learn the truth.

"I will try." Then I turn and hurry inside the house where he can't see me. I don't know how my tone sounded, but what tone can dullen those cutting words? My parents aren't at home, so I flop onto the mat and squeeze my eyes shut, but tears come out anyway. I feel terrible for Vashti. He doesn't deserve to be treated this way. He's in the same boat as I am. He doesn't have a choice in marriage. He's taking it well, and I'm making everything more difficult. Vashti deserves a beautiful, loving wife who would never abandon him. Why can't I be loyal to him? Why can't I love him?

The weekend is awful. My mother pries as to where Vashti is and why he's not with me. My father gives me one angry remark.

"So *this* is how you're going to be married?" I think about what those words mean. No matter how bad I feel for Vashti, I will always want to be rich, and no matter what the man, he will never take that longing away from me. Vashti is a pest, an annoyance, compared to my burning desire to marry someone who can serve me wealth. I can't love anyone incapable of that.

Three

July quickly fades away, and before I know it, August is nearly half-way through. I have three weeks until my wedding. A kind of panic has settled into my stomach. What am I going to do?

I haven't made as much money as I had hoped, but I go to the bank anyway, just to be sure. Every time I stash away some money, my parents take it. My mother doesn't work, so my father requires my financial assistance. When I come to the bank door, Mr Greene waves me in, having just dealt with another customer.

"Hello, Mr Greene. Can I see what's in the account, please?"

"Yes, ma'am." He dives into the vault and comes back with a slit of paper bearing a puny number on it. Only half of what my goals were.

"Mr Greene, do you know where I can work at night or on the weekends?" After considering this for a moment, the banker lights up.

"I know somewhere like that, actually. It pays good, but it's far and goes late into the night."

"What is it?"

"At Seth Sound's castle, the young Prince Ahmir is searching for a wife. They need workers to support their parties. I know Lizzie Kinling goes after school almost every night *and* on the weekends. She makes wonderful money, so I hear."

I smile to myself. Even stepping into the castle would increase my status. I wonder how to get the job. Mr Greene rustles around with papers until he finds one with all the information I need. It's a flier, an advertisement for workers.

"Thank you, sir, very much." I dash out of the building. The sun blazes down, and I'm covered in sweat when I get home.

"Hello, Mother," I greet the woman counting the bills. She only smiles back faintly, but my father answers for her.

"Did you go to the bank, Ed?"

"Yes. I think I've found a new job for nights and weekends." The opportunity interests my mother.

"What is it?" she asks, looking me in the face now.

"Well, it's a bit far, and I would get back late, but it's at the castle." This doesn't have the desired impression. My father is entirely against the king and his End Raiders and won't hear of it. My mother is shocked by the idea of me going to night parties and is concerned about the safety of being out so late.

It takes all of my persuasive skills to get their consent, and even then, they seem reluctant. Finally, however, the need for money wins out.

I apply for the position, and a man, Guava, explains everything to me. The castle employees get to ride on the train for free. It travels to the castle in less than two hours, which is impressive considering how far it is. School dismisses at 2:00, so I can arrive by four and work until ten on school nights. My shift goes until midnight on weekends, but it's just as well. More hours mean more money.

Guava runs the castle's staff. He hands me a red dress to wear at work with matching heels.

"What is it I need to do?"

"You'll be a server, mainly."

My first night on the job comes quickly. I teach the school as usual, except I bring a bag containing my work dress, which is more of a party dress, and my heels. The kids are well-behaved; even my worst students get through their lessons well.

I dismiss school a few minutes early because I don't want to be late on my first day. I slip into my flashy red dress and shoes. The heels make navigating particularly challenging, and I'm wobbling onto the train like I'm on stilts. I've seen heels before, but I've never worn them. I had no idea they were so tricky.

Lizzie Kinling sits alone on the train. I don't like Lizzie much, but I know her. We are the only two people in this compartment, but many more compartments exist. When I sit next to her, Lizzie turns to me, surprised.

"Chapel? I didn't know you work at the castle now. Are you double working?" She says that as if it's an awful thing.

"Oh, I guess, but not really. School is a cinch, and this gig shouldn't be hard," I shrug. I don't want Lizzie to know how desperate I am for money when she has so much of it.

"I don't blame you." She leans close to my ear. "I like money too." Then she giggles as if that's the funniest thing ever. I smile faintly. It won't get me anywhere to be enemies with Lizzie. Being friends with town kids has advantages, especially if I become friends with the Kinlings' daughter.

When the train stops, Lizzie tosses her blond curls over her shoulder. She stands up in her heels with ease and briskly walks off the train. For a second, I'm confused. How can we have arrived so soon? We've only been on for a few minutes.

Then I see Lizzie hop back on with a man walking beside her. The man is wearing a leather jacket, a neatly pressed white shirt, and dress pants. He's smoking a fancy cigar and muttering something to Lizzie. He's definitely rich, far richer than her. Nobody smokes cigars as fancy as those unless they come from the government.

He sits with Lizzie in a different compartment than me. I can't see them, but I hear them talking a bit. For a long time, I ponder what I have seen and wonder what trick Lizzie's pulling this time.

When the train finally stops at the castle, I hobble off like an old lady, but as soon as I've come off the steep incline of the stairs, I try to get a sturdy grip on the ground. I end up half-marching to the castle doors.

There is a tag on my dress stating my name and position. The guard at the door gestures for this, so I show it to him. He nods and lets me through. I see Lizzie do the same, but the man sitting with her on the train reaches into his pocket and pulls out what looks like a ticket. The guard accepts it, but instead of looking at it and handing it back, he rips it in half and throws it away. It must be a one-time-use ticket. The man strolls in, where Lizzie and I both wait for him.

"Okay, Justin. I'll change now." Then Lizzie stalks off with her bag to do just that. I don't know what to say to Justin, so I walk away and look for Guava. I find him, and he shows me that meals and beverages have numbers attached. These numbers align with the tables. I match these and give people their food and drinks, wondering if the rest of the night will be this easy.

I take in my surroundings. The castle itself is gorgeous, not to mention gigantic. The walls are lined with paintings, and the whole building is white marble. My heels dig into the lovely woven rug underneath me, which features an intricate design. The tables are made of finished wood with white fabric tablecloth. An orchestra plays slow, beautiful music constructed of string instruments I've never seen before.

The room swells with soft chatter and the occasional laugh. Whenever I see alcohol, it's usually at a rough bar or casino with many drunk men hanging around obnoxiously. Here, tiny shots are served, along with wine and something called cocktails. Civilized guests dine and slowly drink, none acting a fool and everyone being gracious.

I only see youthful girls and older men. There are no boys or middle aged women, only girls to be possible brides and their fathers to be escorts.

I'm putting down a plate of cold shrimp when I spot Lizzie, but this time, she's not wearing the red server dress. She's in a pale pink dress with a metallic shimmer. It is dainty and no doubt overwhelmingly expensive with long, puffed sleeves. Next to her is the rich Justin, who looks like one of the fathers himself. He isn't smoking now, but he snags a server and places an order. I beckon Lizzie over for an explanation.

"Really," she laughs. "You can't expect me to spend all night in that drab old costume and be a petty server."

"Who's the man?"

"Justin is the father of an old friend; we're pretending to be sisters. She'd be here, except she's got a cold."

"Well, what good does that do? Pretending to be someone you aren't."

"Because it's fun," she snaps. "Dressing up, meeting new people, seeing the prince every night- it's just for a good time."

"So why do you come in pretending to be a server and then transform into some rich man's daughter?"

"Well," she says, blushing for the first time. "For one thing, my parents don't know about Justin and would never permit me. For another, I like the extra money." I marvel at Lizzie's need for money, wanting more even though she already has so much.

"You're engaged to Vashti Marlow." It seems more of an accusation than anything. "My mother told me. He's rather, well, poor, isn't he?"

"He lives in town," I snap, though I don't know why I'm getting defensive.

"Whatever." She shrugs. "Well, enjoy the party." Even though I'm irritated, I return it.

Everyone goes silent. The hall is still at first, but then the crowd stands and claps. I do, too, but for a second, I don't know why. Then I see him. The prince enters the hall with a bejeweled crown among his gorgeous golden hair. The only thing I know about him is his name: Prince Ahmir of Seth Sound.

He is wearing a magnificent forest green robe, with a white shirt, a purple velvet vest, and black pants covered by the robe. He is somewhat short with bright green eyes and a beautiful face. His skin is clear and perfect, not a flaw in sight. He strides by like a prancing lion, and all the girls curtsy in their lavish gowns, and the men bow.

When he gets to me, I can only bend my knees, as I never learned to curtsy, and the dress is too tight around my thighs anyway. I look stupid and clumsy, but it doesn't matter. He barely even looks at me because I'm just a server.

Prince Ahmir greets people, and I continue my duties, though I never take my eyes off Ahmir for too long. I have always heard he looks stunning, but nothing like *this*. When his head turns to the light, the yellow curls flash ruby red for a second before returning to their golden sparkle.

I glimpse him speaking to Lizzie when something happens. One moment, I'm clicking in my heels, holding Table 63's drinks, and the next, I feel myself collide into something. I'm knocked off balance and fall forward. I'm sprawled on the ground, two inches from another girl's face. Her expression is initially terrified, then angry. I realize that while I have been daydreaming, I have run into what is possibly the future queen of Seth Sound. Drink soaks both of us, and the shattered glass lies to my right.

Everyone in the vicinity stares at us, gasping and muttering. Four men pull up the now-sobbing girl and try to clean the front of her dress with napkins. Nobody bothers about me, though many shoot glares in my direction. I frantically search for the prince with my eyes. He's twenty feet away, obviously trying to control his laughter.

Lizzie stands nearby, looking both shocked and sympathetic. I wipe myself down with a rag, though I certainly didn't take the worst of the splatter. I pick up the glass pieces and throw them away. As I clean the floor, I barely suppress tears. It's 6:30 on my first day, and already I've messed things up.

Guava comes over to me, shaking his head.

"That's your only warning. Next time you will be fired."

"I'm so sorry, sir. Really, I'm very sorry."

"Never mind, Miss Chapel. Just don't call any more attention to yourself."

I don't look at the prince anymore and do my duties meekly. I see the girl I knocked over sitting at a table, dabbing her puffy red eyes. I try to give her an apologetic look, but she only scowls and hides her face behind a drenched handkerchief.

By 10:00, I'm exhausted and have to shuffle back to the train. Lizzie's already there, still in her pink dress, with Justin sitting by her.

"Really," she starts up. "What were you thinking?" I swallow my defensiveness and reply evenly.

"I wasn't paying attention." She sighs and shakes her head.

"That's evident. At least you didn't get fired." A small silence follows this.

"How long have you been going to the parties?" I change the conversation.

"Two weeks. Some of the same people come, but I see new faces every time, and most girls only come a couple of nights before they get rejected." I nod, wondering how it feels to be rejected by the prince of Seth Sound. I hope they don't deny the girl I bumped into because of me.

We spend the rest of the ride in silence. Lizzie mutters a thank you to Justin as he leaves the train, and we're the last two in the compartment. The train only stops one more time before we're back in our town. We say goodnight and walk home. Me to my poor village home, her to her rich townhouse.

Four

The next night at the castle, I avoid eye contact with everyone, and I can't stand to even look at the prince as he comes prancing out in a red robe.

I spend the whole night staring at my heels as I go around. Lizzie Kinling has on a shimmering silver dress that I know isn't hers, and then I see another shorter girl in the same dress. I deem it to be Justin's actual daughter, the girl pretending to be Lizzie's sister.

I go home in low spirits, just as I had the night before. I'm so embarrassed about what happened last night that I haven't stopped thinking about it since. Coming inside the house, my mother notices my distress.

"What's the matter?" she asks with a curious look.

"Nothing," I dismiss her and immediately lie on my bed.

I go to sleep quickly, but my dreams are troubled, filled with terrified girls and lions who can laugh, and they laugh at me.

When I wake, it's too early to begin getting ready for school, so I get up and walk into town. Some of the shops are still closed for the night, but there are a few that are just opening. Before I know it, I'm standing outside the repair shop. Vashti is sweeping the steps, humming as usual.

"Good morning, Edelweiss," Vashti calls out, waving me over. I drag my feet but slowly make my way up the steps.

"Hello, Vashti," I say. He smiles and continues sweeping.

"What are you up to?" he teases me. "Not causing trouble, are you?"

"No," I say in a bored tone, squashing the joke. "I'm just taking a walk." He nods but drops his friendly banter. He sweeps, and I watch. This goes on for a while until he breaks the silence.

"Are you ready for the wedding?" My heartbeat quickens. Our wedding is in two and a half weeks.

"Yeah, a little," I lie. "I mean, of course, mhm." The more I talk, the less convincing it sounds. Vashti sighs and leans on the broom.

"You know, Edelweiss, we're going to be a real happy couple. We are. I'm sure of it." When I look into his determined eyes, I know he means what he says.

"I just wish you could make me love you," I say without any thought behind it, and then I suck in my breath. What made me say it? I expect him to get angry like my father when I disrespect him, but Vashti only turns away from me.

"So do I." Vashti stares at the broom, a frown creased on his forehead.

"I'm trying, Vashti," I whisper, feeling horrible about what I said.

"Go home, Edelweiss." His voice stings with hurt.

I turn immediately and storm into the berry patch. Hands against my temple, self-disgust takes over.

"God, what is wrong with me?" I yell to the bushes. "Why can't I just be content?" I break into tears.

A few minutes later, I get ready for school: making breakfast for my parents, putting my hair up, pulling on a white blouse and cornflower blue skirt that hangs over my shoe tops, but all the while, my red eyes threaten to spill over again.

The dreadful, guilty feeling still consumes me. Why can't I love him properly? I surely don't hate him; I feel so terrible for injuring him, but it simply cannot be love that I feel. How I wish it were. Maybe I'm only angry at him because he's not rich, but that sounds so hideous I toss it out of my mind.

As usual, I walk in the grass to town and enter the schoolhouse to ring the bell. My face has returned to its normal color and appearance. The kids pile in, the older ones following Miss Golden into the second room of the schoolhouse, the little ones staying with me. I realize that all the boys playing outside are sweating harder than usual, and the girls are fanning themselves with their textbooks.

Even though it is late August, the sun is peeking in temperature, and the schoolhouse is sweltering with the sheer heat of it. Within half an hour of teaching, my blouse clings to my back.

"World History 1, please." Three girls and two boys pant as they walk to my desk.

"Mary, what were the seven kingdoms of the Realm called before the End Raiders took over?"

"Continents."

"Yes, very good. Now, can each of you tell me the name of a kingdom?"

"Seth Sound."

"Ginger Holmes."

"Le Beth."

"Cap."

"High Fire."

"Chan Hinge."

"Bridger."

"Very good," I praise them. "Now, Thomas, please tell me the kingdom that is the End Raider's homeland."

"I don't know, Miss Chapel."

"Laura?"

"Chan Hinge," she answers proudly.

"Clark, can you tell me the continent name of Chan Hinge?"

"Africa," he mutters after wiping sweat off his forehead.

"Gimmeroy, tell me the continent name of our home kingdom, Seth Sound."

"Asia," she replies before Miss Golden enters the room.

"Edelweiss, dismiss the students please. Due to the weather, we'll call off school for the day." All the kids grin and immediately gather their things.

It's times like these that I wish we could go back to before the End Raiders took over, back to when the Realm was called Earth, and there were precious inventions like the one that makes buildings cool. Alas, when the End Raiders took over, destruction came to the world, and those inventions were lost. Due to massive book burnings, only a handful of these inventions still have instructions, and people these days have no drive to invent new things.

I see only my father when I come home, and I explain that it is just too hot for the kids to learn. I think about all of the marble in the castle where I work. I imagine how comfortable the prince and his family must be, sheltered from the heat.

I do some chores around the house for a while, but then I just put a cool cloth on my forehead and lie down, though I don't sleep. Soon, it's time to change into the red dress I wear every night and take the train to the castle. The train is hot, too, and I soon get a headache. After the two-hour ride, I'm dizzy from the day's constant heat and dehydrated since I haven't drunk water for hours.

I wobble in my heels as I get off the train with Justin, his daughter, and Lizzie. I see black spots before my eyes, but I try to focus on how refreshing it will feel to step inside the cool vicinity of the marble castle. There's a line to get in, and someone's holding it up.

Lizzie, Justin, and his daughter start to swim in my vision, and my throat suddenly goes parched. I can feel myself swaying, but I don't attempt to stop. A wild urgency to get inside overtakes me, but my legs seem to stop moving.

Lizzie moves forward, and the line resumes its usual pace, but I stand still. The black spots get thicker, and my head spins. People are moving in front of me, skipping me in line. Suddenly, I'm falling, and the black spots take over. I collapse, and the last thing I feel is a sharp pain in my head.

My next memory is hazy. I'm lying on a couch, and a young girl speaks softly to me, but I can't quite reach the voice to tell what she's saying. My head hurts, and I want to go back to sleep, so I do.

The next time I wake up, I feel water trickling down my chin. A rag is pressed to my lips, and the refreshing liquid is squeezed out, sliding down my dry throat. I flutter my eyes, but the light is so blinding I close them again. This is the first time that I feel truly awake since I fell.

"Miss?" a woman's voice asks. I grunt in reply. The woman's voice begins to flutter in excitement. "She's awake, she is!" I force my eyes open just as a crowd of five maids charge forward and examine me. They wear identical gray and white uniforms, and their smiles are eager to see me.

"Oh, you *are* pretty!" one of them exclaims. I squint and blink, my eyes agitated.

"Poor dear," the oldest one sighs, combing the hair out of my face. The maids help me sit up, and I take in my surroundings. I'm on a green velvet bed in a large green room decorated entirely green.

"Where am I?" I ask. The maids beam at me.

"You're in the Green Room, Miss. You fainted near the castle and hit your head pretty good."

"How long ago was that?"

"About a day and some ago. The dear princesses have been visiting you a lot."

"The princesses?" I echo. "Am I in the castle?"

"Well, Miss," the elderly one says. "I'm afraid I'll have to tell you the truth. The dear prince has been having such trouble finding a wife that we thought we'd help him out a bit. When Rebecca saw you'd collapsed, we knew we'd have to take you in. We couldn't ruin the opportunity of making a bride out of you, so we told him you're a rich man's daughter living in a country villa. The prince visited you last night, and I never saw him so struck before."

I stare, knowing their lie will only get us all in trouble. What they've done reminds me of Lizzie Kinling's lie.

"That's horrible," I declare. "Shame on you, meddling with what's not your place. I have to tell him the truth right now."

"Oh dear," they mutter. "I'm afraid the girl's right." As I sit up, I realize I'm wearing lavender pajamas in the replacement of my red server's dress. Of course, the dress would have given away to the prince that I'm a server and not a rich girl attending his balls.

I stand up but immediately feel woozy, probably because of my head injury. The maids grab me by the arms and guide me to the door of the Green Room.

It's not until now that I realize the severity of my situation. I have led the eldest prince of Seth Sound to believe that I may marry him and that I intend to do so. The maids steer me down a hallway and into a room decorated in all yellow. Two little girls read on a couch almost identical to the one I slept on, except for the color, and someone else speaks from the corner. It's the prince's voice.

"Ah, dear Ahmir," the elderly maid breathes. "How are you faring, your highness?" Ahmir smiles.

"I am well, Miss Catoline."

"And your sisters?" The reading girls perk up. They must be the twin princesses, Maddy Grace and Maddy Jane. They both close their books, give a polite answer, stand, and courtesy before leaving the room. The maids file out after them, leaving Ahmir and me alone in the Yellow Room.

"Our guest is awake," he says to the room.

"Yes, thank you ever so much for your hospitality, your highness," I almost beg him.

"It's my pleasure. Have a seat." He puts an arm around me and guides me to the couch where his sisters had been. Ahmir sits next to me, and as he doesn't say anything, I decide that now is the best time to tell the truth.

"Er- your highness- it seems there has been some mistake."

"Oh?"

"Yes, you see, I am in no way the honorable, wealthy young woman you think I am. I am, after all, just a server for your magnificent parties who happened to have an accident." I brace myself for his rage, to demand to know who would lie to him, but instead, he smiles.

"Yes, I know. I knew as soon as I saw you who you were. You're the server who ran into Little Miss Levinia." My face turns crimson. Of course, he'd recognize me after that.

"I must soon go back home to my family. I'm sorry you were deceived." Prince Ahmir sighs.

"Then I must keep searching for a wife."

"May I recommend my friend, Lizzie Kin- Lizzie." I don't know why I say it. I know it might get Lizzie in trouble, and I don't even know her pretend last name. Ahmir raises his eyebrows.

"Lizzie Stoneman?"

"Yes, that's the one," I say eagerly. The prince frowns.

"You prefer her over her sister?"

"I don't know her sister so well," I say smoothly. He seems to toss the whole conversation out of his mind with his following sentence.

"But you must stay awhile. I like company, and yours seems especially good." My cheeks burn, but almost in a nice way.

"Tell me your name," he continues.

"Edelweiss Chapel."

"What does your father do?"

"He's been in the military for eight years."

"He serves the End Raiders?" Ahmir interrupts, delighted.

"Uh, no, actually. He fights against them... and your father." Ahmir considers this for a moment, then brushes it aside.

"It will go without concern," he assures me.

"He doesn't know I'm here," I say, suddenly alarmed. Someone must tell him. My mother is undoubtedly worried sick."

"Why, of course," Ahmir smiles. "Any good mother wouldn't want to lose a child as precious as you." I feel a glow in my stomach, but I shake it off immediately.

"I'm not a good daughter," I inform him.

"Surely you don't believe that," he remarks. "Don't worry about your parents. You may write to them after dinner, but you can't leave yet. You have been injured, and you must rest."

"I feel fine," I lie quickly, even though I'm dizzy, woozy, and famished. At the word *dinner,* I realize my hunger. Ahmir seems to notice this, too.

"We will see after we eat. Come follow me to the dining Room."

Prince Ahmir leads me out of the Yellow Room. The dining Room is filled with tables covered with white tablecloths, each of different sizes. It reminds me of what a fancy restaurant would look like, though I've never been in one. At one table, with three chairs, the twin princesses sit.

"These are my sisters, Maddy Jane and Maddy Grace," Ahmir introduces me.

"It's good to meet you, your Highnesses. I'm Edelweiss," I say. The identical twins have dark hair, deep blue eyes, and fair skin. They wear matching navy blue dresses that fall to their toes.

I feel momentarily awkward because there's only one empty seat, but then Ahmir draws another from a different table, and I sit at it. We only have to wait a minute for a bright orange soup to be served.

"It's so wonderful here," I exclaim, having never been anywhere like this.

"Yes, since my father gained rule of the place, he has certainly outdone himself to ensure our comfort."

"Where *is* your father?"

"Oh," he replies. "My father- he never eats with us, you see. He eats with the business people he works with."

"What's in the soup?" I ask. I notice that Maddie Grace and Maddie Jane are already shoveling it down.

"Pumpkin," he answers. I raise my eyebrows. Three years ago, I got some pumpkin seeds for my thirteenth birthday. The seeds never grew, though, and I had been sorely disappointed. That was the last time I have thought about pumpkins.

"Sounds great," I tell him and pick up my spoon. He does the same, and soon, the pumpkin soup is gone, though its delicious flavor is left in my mouth.

After four more courses of bread and butter, pork, salad, and custard for dessert, I am both stuffed and exhausted. Prince Ahmir sees this and shows me back to the Green Room, where he says goodnight.

"I look forward to seeing you in the morning," he says. Then he turns away. "Goodnight, Edelweiss," he calls over his shoulder as I enter the

Green Room. I stumble onto the couch and pile blankets and pillows around me. I'm so warm and snug I never want to leave. I never want to go back to the town to sweat in that stuffy classroom, even if the heatwave is over.

Nobody has ever treated me the way Ahmir has: not Vashti, not my mother, nobody. Vashti has no money, no prospects, no future. What does he want with me? And my parents don't give me their affection, not even the freedom to choose my own husband. I would do anything to cast my old life out the window. To be rid of Vashti, my father, and even my mother would hardly be a sacrifice. I would be happy with Prince Ahmir. And happiness is something I have never really felt to my satisfaction.

Am I greedy to think such things? I convince myself I'm not. I'm meant to live this new life. I know I am because, for the first time in my life, love has found me.

Five

The following day, Ahmir supplies me with paper and an ink pen, something I've never used before. I write to my mother first:

Dear Mother,
I'm at the castle with the prince. I had an accident, and I'm sorry if you were worried about me. I don't know when I'll be home.

I sign my name and then write to my father.

Hello Father,
I am with Prince Ahmir at his castle. He invited me to stay a while, and I accepted. The date of my return journey is yet to be decided. I hope my letter finds you well and you wait patiently for my homecoming.
Edelweiss Chapel

I hesitate before I write to my fiance. How do I want to come across? Kind? Sorry? Angry? Cold? I'm still going to marry him, so I am apologetic.

Vashti,
I hope you think kindly of me when you read this. I'm sorry if I scared you by not returning from work. There's been an accident, and I am recovering from an injury. Please keep my parents company while I'm away. I'm in good hands.

The letters seem short, but there's nothing more to say. I put all three of them in one envelope, and Ahmir takes care of the rest.

I join the prince and his sisters for breakfast. There is a highchair where the baby prince eats his meal this time.

"What's his name?"

"Livingston," Ahmir says as a server puts porridge in front of us. "Do you have any siblings, Edel?"

"No, but I'm engaged." Ahmir goes quiet, and I can see in his face that his agenda does not fit Vashti into the plan.

"When will you be married?" he asks finally once we finish eating.

"In two weeks. Though- I don't want to be!" I burst out. He gazes at me curiously.

"Why are you then?"

"Vashti- that's my fiance- has been forced upon me. My parents arranged our marriage, but I don't want it." Tears spill into my eyes now. "I don't know what to do. I don't even have remote feelings for him, and he's so poor." Ahmir considers this.

"Maddie Jane, Maddy Grace, will you take Livingston upstairs for his nap?" The twins hurry out of the room with their baby brother. The room seems oddly huge, with only Ahmir and me filling the space. "Have you told your parents this?"

"Yes," I sob, tears trickling down my face.

"And they don't care?" he asks in amazement.

"Not enough to call off the wedding. My mother says I'll get used to him."

"Then you should stay here."

"Do you mean it?" I ask, bewildered.

"Here," he says, handing me a handkerchief. I dab my puffy, red eyes with it. "Now then, you'll just stay here for a while, and we'll figure it all out later." I smile weakly and wipe away my tears. When we stand up, he puts his arm around me again.

"Thank you," I whisper, and we go to the Yellow Room, where the girls are waiting.

"My sisters love to play games," Ahmir informs me. "Do you?"

"I've never played real games before, actually," I say with brighter spirits.

"Really? Well, then, we'll have to teach you some." Maddie Jane introduces me to a game called Checkers, which she says has been around for centuries. Maddie Grace and Ahmir show me an outdoor court where we play a game known as Ping Pong. We all laugh and play and have a good time, something I haven't done in ages, if ever. My parents don't play, and I never roughhoused with the schoolboys.

Even though we have no protection against the summer heat, it isn't too bad, and we don't care. Thankfully, the horrid heatwave is over.

When we finally go back inside for lunch, Maddie Grace holds my hand. I smile. I like Ahmir's sisters very much.

Lunch is warm ham in a pineapple sauce. There's also a fruit salad and cornbread. I've never eaten such a good lunch in my life. Most days, I eat only a slice of bread at noon, nothing like this. When we finish, Ahmir shows me to the castle's library, where there are thousands of books, mostly old ones, but new ones also. After the End Raiders' book burnings, most books were lost, and hardly anybody writes new ones now. Ahmir shows me some of his favorites, primarily written in the nineteenth century.

"This one was written last year." He points to a small book titled, "The Girl With the Dresses."

"What's it about?" I ask.

"I don't know. I haven't read it, but it's probably about a girl with dresses."

"I think you're on the right track," I laugh.

"But don't take my word for it," he says. "You should read it. Tell me if I'm right."

"Really?"

"Of course! No need for it to sit around here and get dusty."

"You like books, don't you, Ahmir?"

"I love them."

"Do you write at all?"

"No, I don't have the creativity, I guess, but my father's a poet." I had not known this about the king. "Do you do anything of the kind?"

"No, I didn't get the proper education."

"I bet you have the loveliest voice."

"No," I giggle. "Not me."

"Well, there must be something. I know! You should dance."

"Oh no. I don't even know the first thing."

"Come on," he coaxes. "Try with me." He convinces me to let him teach me and hums a tune to dance to. I know I'm awful, but he sends only his compliments and teaches me a couple of basic kinds. Then he spins me around and around, and soon I'm dizzy. I fall into his arms, laughing, until I regain my balance.

"Do you like dancing now?" Ahmir asks, also laughing.

"Oh yes!" I say breathlessly. "Though I never thought I would enjoy it at all." He grins.

"I've got another party in an hour. How would you like to be the special guest of honor?" I hesitate. What if people recognize me as the server who collided with the young lady? Ahmir sees my concern.

"Don't worry, Edel. Once the maids get hold of you, you'll be unrecognizable."

"Alright," I say, and it turns out he's right. The maids curl my hair, french braid a section, and twist it into a knot on the back of my head. They place a gold headband and a matching necklace on me. They apply makeup, something I've never experienced before, and dress me in a beautiful gown of pink silk.

When Prince Ahmir sees me, he exclaims that I look stunning. So does he, I notice, though I only thank him. When it's time, we link arms as we enter the ballroom, where the guests are. Many young women gasp in astonishment when they see the prince with a girl, and one young lady actually starts crying. I feel a glow run through me. Where I was a servant before, I am a prize now. Just by fainting on the doorstep of Seth Sound's castle, I have become the most coveted girl in the kingdom.

The girls look at me in envy as Ahmir and I walk the aisle. Everyone bows, even Lizzie Kinling, whose eyes widen in shock. I beam at Ahmir. His green eyes seem to glow brighter than usual. We hold hands up on the stage, where he usually greets his guests. Tonight, he introduces me.

"Greetings, ladies and gentlemen. Thank you all for coming. As you can see, I have a very pretty young lady here with me. She is the guest of honor for tonight and will be dancing with me." I stifle a gasp. I do not want to make a fool of myself in front of all these people.

We walk down from the stage, and the band plays a slow waltz for us. My hands shake, but I take a deep breath and dance with Ahmir as every eye turns to us. When the song ends, everyone claps. Then, a new song comes on, and they join in. Fathers and daughters dance, each girl hoping that the prince will ask them, but Ahmir doesn't. He doesn't dance with anyone but me the whole night, and soon, my legs start to step with ease, and my dancing improves.

We eat dinner somewhere in the night. It's steak and a strange species of purple potatoes. Around one o'clock, Ahmir and I wave goodbye to the guests and retreat to bed. Although I now know my way to the Green Room, Ahmir leads me there. When we approach the door, he puts his arms around my waist and kisses me. I'm so shocked my whole body seems to go limp for a second.

"Goodnight, my lovely," he whispers and turns to leave. I rest my hand on the door handle, but I don't turn it until I can't hear his footsteps anymore. Then I open the door and climb onto the couch. Wrapping myself in the blanket, I let a smile slip onto my face. The prince of Seth Sound loves me. I'm the happiest girl in the world.

Six

When I get up early in the morning, I find I am the only one awake besides a few servants. I can't sleep, so I wander the halls in my white silk nightgown. I hear footsteps down the hall coming in my direction. At first, it seems to be a maid, but the footfalls are too heavy for one. Soon, I see a scowling man dressed in a red robe striding up to me.

"Who are you?" the man demands, stopping directly in front of me. He has a thickly lined forehead, a tall stature, and a harsh mouth. The only pleasant feature on his severe face is his eyes like green gems.

"I'm Edelweiss Chapel," I introduce myself to the red-robed man.

"I don't want your name. What are you doing here?" he snaps.

"I suppose I'm a girl recovering from injury," I answer, unsure how to reply. The man looks perplexed.

"This is not a hospital. Why are you here?"

"The prince said I could stay," I stammer.

"The prince? Ahmir?"

"Yes, sir, he has been kind to me, and I am very grateful." Suddenly, the man takes on a whole different attitude.

"He wants you to stay? Does he want you wandering the halls at this hour without an escort? Go back to bed, girl." His voice is gentler, almost excited. I obey immediately and hasten to leave the red-robed man. I sit on the green couch, wondering who he is. Who is this man who thinks he's of such power and yet does not reveal his identity?

I get up again when I hear the mutter of voices and footsteps. I go to the Dining Room, where I find Ahmir, Maddie Grace, Maddie Jane, and Livingston waiting.

"Good morning Edelweiss," Ahmir greets me.

"Good morning," I repeat. The server puts potatoes, biscuits, and gravy on our plates.

"How did you sleep?" The prince spears a potato with his fork.

"Very well." My reply is automatic, but then I hesitate. Should I tell him about my encounter? I am about to, but then I catch Ahmir's green eye. It is the exact color and shape of the man's eyes. I realize that I have just met King Roe, Ahmir's father. I decide not to mention it.

After breakfast, we take a walk in the gardens. It's stunningly beautiful, and there are so many plants. Ahmir shows me a spot with little white flowers.

"Edelweiss," I exclaim in delight, recognizing the flower I was named after.

"I thought you might like that," he says, putting an arm around me. We just stand there, taking in the garden's beauty and the edelweiss, until we hear his sisters coming up behind us. We hold hands as we walk through the landscape, the girls taking turns smelling every flower and deciding on their favorite.

We have such a good time in the garden that we don't spot a rain cloud coming in until it's pouring down on us. Laughing and screaming, we cover our heads with our hands and run into the castle. The rain comes down slowly and seems to put a spell of languor on us. We sit and stare out the window, still dripping from the rain. Eventually, the little girls give up on sitting still and run off to play with their dolls.

I sit beside Ahmir on the couch, resting my head on his shoulder. He strokes my hair as we stare at the rainy window, where a gusty breeze shakes the trees.

"I love you," Ahmir murmurs. The only time I've ever heard those words spoken to me was by Vashti, but that hardly counts. When Ahmir says it, a warm feeling rushes through me, and I hold onto his arm.

"I love you too." I have never said that before.

At lunchtime, we lethargically get up and go to the dining hall. It's lamb chops and mint jelly, something the prince and princesses always eat, but I've never had.

After lunch, Ahmir tells us he has to attend a meeting that may last a few hours. I keep the girls busy for as long as possible while they show me their expensive china dolls. Each one has a name and personality, and they seem so life-like to me. Then we play a game called Pattycake that they teach me, which is silly and pointless: all you do is chant a rhyme and make motions with your hands. Neither pastime takes much time, and though it's no longer raining, it's too wet to go outside.

The girls get busy playing with Baby Livingston, so I just wander the hallways again. This time, I hear voices coming from a door, one of which is the rough tones of the red-robed man I suspect to be the king.

"You must ask her soon."

"Why her?" another voice calls, and I realize it's Ahmir.

"I thought you said you like her," accuses the red-robed man.

"I do, Father, but she's nothing special, and I've only just met her." This confirms my suspicions. The red-robed man is the Raiders' king.

"Ahmir, the truth is you have to get married soon. The public doesn't think well enough of the End Raiders. They think we're cruel and heartless. They don't want to serve a widower who is accused of murdering his wife."

"You didn't murder Mother. She drowned," Ahmir mutters.

"But it's all about the image. People want someone fresh, someone new. They want a wedding."

"But I'm not ready to marry."

"Why not, Ahmir?"

"I don't know." He hesitates before continuing. "Ever since Mother died, I figured marriage isn't worth the pain."

"Ahmir," King Roe starts again, though his voice is much softer. "Sometimes you have to take that risk."

"But why can't I do something else to help with the End Raiders? What if I traveled to the kingdoms and talked to everyone. I could rally support that way."

"You can talk to them all you want, Ahmir, but actions and not words will gain their support. Show them your dedication by marrying."

"Please don't make me, Father. Give me more time. I'm only eighteen. My mother died less than a year ago. Can't you see I'm not ready?"

"You are very mature for your age, Ahmir. You are more ready than you think you are."

"Do you really want me to marry a sixteen-year-old?"

"Better sixteen than sixty. She's young, pretty, and willing, isn't she?" There's a pause.

"Yes, I think so," Ahmir says finally, evidently defeated.

"Well then, you'll ask her today."

"What?" Astonishment rings through Ahmir's voice.

"Today, Ahmir. If you don't hurry up, we will lose people's support. A show must be put on, or we may lose the war."

"But Father," Ahmir argues.

"No, Ahmir. I'm tired of your excuses. Since you can't find a suitable wife on your own, I have chosen one for you." Ahmir sighs, and I hear them stand up. I dash away, quickly and quietly, into the Green Room to digest what I just learned. The first thought that comes through my head is this:

Another arranged marriage. I will always be in an arranged marriage.

But there is something that doesn't make sense. "She's nothing special," Ahmir had said. Why has he been treating me as he has been if he doesn't think I'm special? Why was I his guest of honor? Why did he kiss me? Has it all been just an act?

Ahmir betrayed me. I trusted him, and now he thinks he can manipulate me into marrying him for his father's sake.

How should I answer? Should I deny him? Should I go back to my little unnamed village and marry Vashti Marlow? Or maybe I should stay with Ahmir anyway, with his great fortune and status. These thoughts are all so complicated; I just want to lie down and cry, yet no tears come to me.

Someone knocks on my door, startling me. I compose my face and open the door. Ahmir stands there, smiling.

"Should we go to dinner, then? I'm sorry that took so long, by the way."

"No problem," I say faintly. We walk to the Dining Room together, but I can feel a chill in the air. The girls are already there, with Livingston sitting in his highchair between them. We don't talk but only eat our roast beef and cooked carrots. During our meal, I decide how I will answer Ahmir.

After dinner, we eat a peach cobbler and head to bed. Ahmir walks me there, as usual, but the atmosphere is entirely different. I expect him to get down on one knee at any moment. Now I panic. Am I making the right choice?

"How's your head feeling?" he asks once we're at the door.

"I can hardly even tell it was injured," I reply, for I haven't felt its effects for a couple of days.

"That's wonderful," he says, though neither of us see anything wonderful happening. He doesn't love me and is just as miserable as I was with Vashti. I decide not to wait until he asks me. I just tell him the truth.

"I overheard you talking to your father," I admit.

"How much did you hear?" he mutters, staring at the floor.

"Enough to know what you intend to do, but I must go home. I can't stay with you forever. Not like this."

"My father-".

"I understand," I lie because I don't understand his pretenses at all. He stares at my face as if searching for something to say but turns away a second later.

"Goodnight, Edelweiss." He leaves, and a potent desire seizes me to take back my answer- to stay with him.

I am marrying Vashti and not Ahmir. That's what pains me. At least Vashti doesn't pretend to love me. I think Vashti actually does.

The next day is heart-wrenching. I eat breakfast, though I can hardly taste the eggs and sausage patties. Ahmir tells me I should get ready to leave. The maids bring me the red dress I wore the night I fainted, which seems to have been ages ago. I wish someone would just sit down and explain why everybody does what they do.

I don't have any of my own items with me, so there's nothing to pack. I wait on the castle steps for the noon train. I feel sick to my stomach. I thought I was getting rid of my old life, and now, I will marry Vashti in a week. The most I can hope for is that I can postpone the wedding due to my injuries.

Ahmir comes up from behind me, and I can see that he is miserable, too, probably because he has to face his father's disappointment at my refusal.

"Goodbye, Edelweiss. I'm sorry for the trouble I've caused you." I don't say anything, but I nod, and he leaves. The train comes, and I get on it back to my little, unnamed village. The ride doesn't seem to take long enough, and I'm frightened my family will ask me many questions I don't want to answer.

I get off the train, only to find Lizzie Kinling waiting to get on. She's wearing a silver dress, not the red server one.

"Where are you going?" I ask.

"To the castle, silly," she giggles, beaming.

"For work? Don't you have school today?"

"Edelweiss, you *have* heard, right?"

"Heard what? Did something happen to the school?" I frown in confusion. Lizzie laughs as if it's the funniest thing ever.

"I'm marrying the prince, duh. I got his letter this morning." I don't say anything; my mind is working too fast. My whole world is turning upside down, but suddenly, it makes sense. I nod and hurriedly leave Lizzie so I can work it all out.

I meander to my house so I have time to think everything through. I realize that I misinterpreted Ahmir's conversation with his father. He and King Roe must have been talking about Lizzie, not me. Now that I think about it, they never said my name, yet I concluded they were talking about me. That means that when I refused him, I wasn't really refusing him because he wasn't asking to marry me. I smile briefly at the thought that Ahmir had said Lizzie "wasn't anything special."

In my first conversation with the prince, I told him that Lizzie was a good friend of mine and would make a suitable partner. Maybe it is my fault after all that Ahmir is marrying her.

But why is Ahmir's father, King Roe, choosing Lizzie? Maybe it is simply that he thinks she is good-looking, as he had mentioned to Ahmir. Or perhaps he favors her pretend father, Justin. That seems likely. I know that Justin has to be in the government because of the way he wears and smokes his money.

I realize the misery of my situation. Ahmir and I want to marry each other, but Ahmir's forced to marry Lizzie, and I'm forced to marry Vashti. Lizzie will be the only happy one, and she's the one who's been deceiving Ahmir. The world is not a fair place.

The house looks the same as always, and my mother greets me at the door, flinging her slender arms around me.

"Oh, Edelweiss! Finally, you're home. I've been so worried about you."

"Yeah, it's okay now. It's all okay."

My mother laughs breezily, not noticing my agitation.

"Do you want some lunch?"

"No, can I just lay down for a bit? It's been a long day." I lay down on the mat beside my parent's bed. It's not half as comfortable as the couch in the Green Room, but I'm used to it. I watch the sunset from the little window in the room. It reminds me of all my hopes, dreams, desires, wishes, whatever you want to call it, sinking deep beneath the horizon, unreachable.

My father comes home, and we have dinner: a loaf of bread, dried meat, and some berries. I sigh, wishing for the real dinner I had at the castle. How I long to be rich. The good fortune was so close to being in my grasp, but now I let it slip through my fingers like sand at the beach.

My father jokes throughout dinner, but one particular gibe gets my attention.

"For a while there, I thought you ran away with the prince, Ed. It's good to see your head's not in the cloud like he is." The remark sparks my temper, the temper I inherited from my father.

"Ahmir's not *in the clouds*," I mutter through clenched teeth and a mouthful of bread.

"I'm sorry, what did you say? Has the prince struck you dumb? Speak up, girl." Speak up, I do.

"I know why you're doing this," I accuse him, standing up. "You're so prejudiced against the End Raiders, you forget they're even human."

"No, that princeling is so steeped in royal steam that he gave up his humanity long ago. He thinks he can rule the whole Realm, just like his wretched father."

"How dare you insult Ahmir!" I shriek. "You, with nothing. You poor, obscure, miserable villager. You have no work, you live in a shack, and you contain your own daughter from greatness. You're one to talk about what Ahmir can and can't do."

"You will be silent," my father bellows.

"Edelweiss, please," my mother begs. "You may have been exposed to other cultures at that castle, but you are not exempt from using your manners here."

"You idiots," I bawl. "To care about table manners. You don't even know what almost came your way. Even a blind squirrel finds a nut eventually, but only a stupid squirrel buries it."

"Have you lost your mind?" My father grabs my wrist and yanks me toward him. "After all I've taught you, you've been brainwashed by three days with those power-hungry mules."

"I'm hungry because you have starved me. Look at me! I'm not even allowed to choose my own husband. How's that for *power*?" I spit at him.

"I have carefully paved a path of success for you, and this is how you repay me?" he yells. I snatch my wrist back, stride to the door, and yank it open. I slam it on my way out and turn, running into the berry patch and tearing past it.

How far does the world go? The faster I run, the less tormented I feel. But eventually, I stumble. I don't get up again until morning, despite the pain in my heart.

Seven

I wake up to a faint clopping sound, not like the rain that poured down steadily all night, but like horse hooves. I feel miserable: unable to control my shivers, soaked to the bone, and with a tremendous headache. I should have anticipated it; after all, I did spend the whole night in a muddy berry patch in the rain.

The clopping sound gets louder, and then I see two brown horses pulling a buggy. I sit up, though my stiff bones protest. I groan and rub my grimy face with mud-covered hands. Then I gasp because the horses are charging toward me, and their speed nearly propels the buggy into the air. Through the berry patch, those horses trample, their reckless driver shouting encouragement at them. Soon, the buggy is right behind me. I crawl toward it and wave my arms until the driver stops the horses.

"You need a lift?" a gravelly voice asks. I hesitate, but I do need a ride. It's unlikely anyone else will come through and offer, and my body is certainly not up for a long hike. I can't stay here, either, or I'll be found and brought back home. I can't go back home; I just can't.

"Yes, please," I consent, hoisting myself beside the person. I see by his overalls that it is a man and by the wrinkles beneath his large straw hat, a very old one. "Thank you, sir," I say. "Where are you going?"

"The post office," he replies. "But don't call me sir."

"What should I call you?"

"Your majesty will do." I stare at the old man. He removes his hat to reveal a bun of gray hair and an elderly woman's face. "My name is

Queen Lotus of Seth Sound." I stare at her, remembering her from my history class as the queen who abdicated the throne after her husband was shot. This woman is Ahmir's grandmother.

"Your- Your Majesty," I stammer. "I didn't think-"

"Didn't think I'd be wearing overalls, like some desperate farmer?"

"I guess not. Why are you disguised like that?"

"It's a dangerous country, lass, as you well know by the looks of your dress there. Seth Sound is a divided kingdom. Some people hate me. They killed my husband, why not me?"

"Forgive me, Your Majesty, but I don't follow the news much. Are you still against the End Raiders?" There's a long silence before Queen Lotus answers.

"I'll never support a single government, but I'm so old, I'll be resting with my dear husband long before that happens. You'll probably be my age by the time the End Raiders pull off a thing like taking over the entire world."

"Yes, my father is very much against the End Raiders. He fought in the war against them for eight years, but I don't care about politics." Lotus snorts.

"Don't care about politics? It ain't about politics, girl; it's about freedom and power. It's a hard thing to balance. You'll see that no one gets any say once there's a single power. You bet your britches it'll be a sorry world, just like last time." I'm taken aback by the abdicated queen's rough language.

"How come your son is the leader of the End Raiders if his parents hated them so much?"

"Don't go blaming me and my late husband now, girl. A family is not like a government. Parents can't dictate their child's lives, now can they?"

"I don't know about that. My parents are forcing me to marry." Lotus shakes her head.

"My grandson, Ahmir, almost met the same fate." My heart seems to stop.

"Almost? What happened?"

"Well, as it turns out, the girl he was going to marry is a fake. She was about to get away with pretending to be the daughter of an End Raider general, Justin Stoneman, but Stoneman's real daughter got jealous and told on her. I've never seen my son so enraged. But Ahmir was jumping for joy. He and I convinced Roe to let him marry this poor, nobody girl instead, but the trouble is, we don't know where she is. All he knows is that she lives in an unnamed village.

"That's why I'm here. I'm sending a copy of his love letter to every village post office I can find, hoping one will find its way to the damsel. He must love her very much to write the same letter so many times. I've counted at least fifty. It's tedious work, writing letters."

I almost cry out of joy. Ahmir isn't marrying Lizzie, and he does love me after all. I can soon be back with him, and we can be happy forever.

"Is her name Edelweiss Chapel?" I verify, wondering if it's too good to be true.

"Yeah, actually, that sounds about right. You know her?"

"Know her? I *am* her." Lotus stops the horses.

"You mean to tell me you've been letting me jabber on this whole time, and *you* are Miss Chapel?"

"Yes," I cry. "May I read my letter?"

"No, girl, I had distinct orders to deliver these letters to the post offices, not to hobos wearing the dresses we give out to castle servers."

"But you've found me. Can't you just give me a letter?"

"No," says Lotus, and she slaps the horses to go, though I can see a hint of a smile on her wrinkled face.

"Oh, but you have to," I plead.

"I don't have to do anything; I'm a widowed queen. I'm exempt from the rules." I gape at her, then give up. The whole ride to the post office, I expect her to tell me she's joking and give me one of the letters, but she doesn't. When we reach our destination an hour later, she puts back on her hat and hands Ahmir's letter to the man at the post office.

"So long, Miss Chapel," calls Lotus, and she's gone. I think she's the strangest person I've ever met. She talks like a farmer, drives horses like a madman, and is not at all curious about my story or why she found me lying in the mud wearing a server's dress from *her* castle. Her stubborn and insensible refusal to just hand me the letter is the most irritating thing about her.

I walk up to the man at the post office, humiliated by my soiled clothing, and ask for a letter addressed to Edelweiss Chapel. The man frowns.

"That old farmer just delivered one. And he even called out your name."

"Yes, I know, he's rather strange," I explain. "An old family friend."

"I can see that," he mutters and hands over the letter. My heart races as I tear open the envelope. As I do, I wonder if Queen Lotus will still send every copy of the letter to the post offices and waste her time. That's the thing; Lotus isn't an actual queen since she abdicated. I shake off these unimportant thoughts as soon as I can tear open the envelope.

The letter is made from expensive white paper and an ink pen. It reads:

My dearest Edelweiss-

Of all the things I am most sorry for, my deepest regret is letting you go. As you are already aware of, my father was forcing my hand in marriage. However, I want to tell you the truth about Lizzie Stoneman, or should I say Kinling. In fact, the girl isn't even related to the Stonemans, as her fake sister, Ms Eliza Stoneman, informed me. She has been arrested for her deceit and sentenced to a decade in prison. I never had any feelings for her, though it seems like an unjustly harsh punishment.

You are my one and only true love, so come back to me. My father has consented for me to marry you. Please, my dearest, accept my hand in marriage and stay with me forever. Return to the castle as soon as you receive this letter, and I will be there waiting.

Love always,

Ahmir

My eyes sparkle with tears. My energy is renewed, and my wounded heart seems to heal instantly. I have no money, decent clothing, or transportation, only this one letter to get me through.

I grit my teeth and leave the post office. I walk a mile until I find a murky lake to bathe in. My head feels like it will split from the pain, I have bruises from my fall, and my whole body aches. I take off my dress and scrub it as clean as I can. At least the majority of the mud comes off. I wash my hair to some extent in the lake water and put on my soaked dress again. It's torn from last night's run through the shrubbery, and dark grime stains cover it.

I leave the lake, and my dress dries on my way back to the small town. I've never been here before, so I ask a woman with a little girl if there's a train that runs up to the castle.

"Yes," the woman replies simply and steers her daughter away from me. I know I must look hideous, and I don't blame her for distrusting me, but it would have been a help if she had given me a hint as to where I might find that train station. I see a map on a bulletin board to discover the station is half a mile away. Walking there is agony, but I have had painful hikes before. Once I get there, I find a clock that tells me it is eleven forty. I know there is a noon train, so I sit and wait twenty minutes.

Sure enough, a train comes on time, and I stand to get on it. A man steps off the train.

"Ticket, ma'am." He holds out his hand. I dread his words, sensing that this could be a significant problem.

"Oh dear, I forgot about that, sir. As you can see from my dress, though, I am a server at the castle."

"Might want to put that one through the cleaners," the man comments with a smirk. "What time does your shift start? Most girls with your dress don't come until two or three o'clock."

"I mean, I don't work there anymore, but I must see the prince immediately. It's urgent."

"You can buy a ticket at the booth," the man suggests.

"But I don't have any money," I plead.

"Okay, well, I'm not the boss. I can't just *give* you a ticket." I panic. What am I going to do? Then I remember my only possession clamped tightly in my hand.

"I have a letter from the prince to the future princess, with his signature," I offer hastily, showing him my precious letter. He reads it with some level of interest.

"What do you want me to do with it?" he asks.

"It could be worth some money, eventually."

"So, should I just give my boss a letter when he asks for the earnings?" His voice is thick with sarcasm. I sigh.

"Please take it. I have nothing else," I beg, tears beginning to spill from my eyes.

"Sorry, I can't help you," he says, handing back my letter. He walks back on the train and leaves.

I sit on a bench and read through my letter, though a few tears drop onto the paper and smudge the ink. The whole world ignores me. Everyone moves around me as they always do. They avert their eyes from my sobbing.

I sleep on the bench that night, and it becomes apparent that I am sick from the cold rain of the night before. In the morning, the woman at the ticket booth gives me some bread to eat and water to drink. She tells me that train tickets are cheap and to find a job. I knock on people's doors all day, begging for work, but no one needs any services. I even try to sell people my beloved letter, but nobody cares about it except me.

On the third night, I sleep on the bench again. The one thing I never do is let go of Ahmir's letter, and that alone keeps me going.

I get a bad cough, and my headache becomes unbearable. There are no jobs, nobody has money to spare, and I cannot get to my prince. I'm so hungry and thirsty that I might die on this bench.

I struggle to sit up on the third day, and I'm racking my brains for a way, however wild, to get to my prince. The 4:00 train rolls in as usual, and a crowd of passengers spills out. With them is a farmer in overalls. He's an old thing, and even with my weak, blurry eyes, I recognize him, and I know right away this isn't a farmer. Something in me wants to laugh with relief, but my tired body refuses. However frustrating she may be, what a dear thing she is.

"Your majesty," I call, waving. "It's me, Edelweiss." Lotus barely tips her hat to me and continues walking in the same direction, away from me. "Where are you going? Take me to the prince, please."

"I am buying you a train ticket," she explains, slapping money onto the ticket booth. The woman hands a ticket to her.

"Come now, Miss Chapel," Lotus calls to me. I stumble dizzily behind her. We get on the train, and I try to sleep but can't. Ahmir's grandmother feeds me a container of grapes and nothing more, though she has an entire bottle of water and cheese danish.

"Can I have some of that?" I ask.

"No," she snaps, hugging the danish to her chest. "These are my favorites. If you wanted one, why didn't you bring one?" I just shake my head in disbelief. There's no arguing with a queen like her.

The train finally stops at the castle, but I can hardly breathe from my elation. I can't fathom how wonderful it will be to be with Ahmir again and to finally be in good hands. After the last three days, I never want to leave the castle again.

I go up the castle steps, barefoot, next to Lotus. The butler opens the door, and we step inside.

"Prince Ahmir is in the Yellow Room," the butler informs us. Before leaving, the queen tells me to take a bath before greeting Ahmir.

I heed her advice and soak in a tub of hot water for at least half an hour. My burning desire to get to Ahmir eventually forces me to get out of the warm water. Pulling on a soft, baby blue dress, I experience comfort once more, for the first time since I left the castle.

I make my way down the hall until I'm right outside the Yellow Room. I hear one of the twins speaking, and Ahmir murmurs something back. He sounds discouraged. I wonder if they're talking about me. I take a deep breath, knock on the door, and turn the handle.

Maddie Grace turns her head to me and her face lights up immediately.

"Edelweiss!" she shrieks.

Ahmir looks too surprised and relieved to say anything, but he holds his arms out to me. I throw myself into him, and it is without question the happiest moment of my life. I rest my head against his neck, and he hugs me so tight I think I might burst.

"You can't even know how I've missed you," I whisper to Ahmir.

"You won't ever leave again, do you hear?"

"Never. Why would I? I've gotten terribly sick. I will have to tell you all about my troubles these past few days, but I'm so famished. Have you had dinner yet?"

"No, but we will eat in the Green Room so you can lie down. You don't look well at all." He helps me walk there, as I'm so dizzy and light-headed I can hardly stand on my own. I throw myself onto the couch but then grimace because my body aches so bad.

The maids bring hot tea and dinner into the Green Room, and while we eat, I tell Ahmir everything that went on, right down to the fight I had with my father. I don't exclude a single detail because I want Ahmir to know everything. He was especially shocked when I told him I misinterpreted his conversation with his father. Afterwards, Ahmir tells me his story.

"It hadn't been an hour since you left the castle that Rosa Stoneman confessed Lizzie's secret, and I knew I had to get you back. Lizzie arrived at the castle expecting to marry me and instead received a prison sentence. My father was so wrathful; I had never seen him so angry. My father cannot stand to be tricked."

"That's awful," I say, imagining the scowling, red-robed man in a fit of temper. "I knew about Lizzie being a Kinling; she lives in my town. But I never thought it would do any harm, especially not something like this. Her family must be devastated." Ahmir nods.

"It doesn't sound right, but it was wonderful for me. I knew that as soon as Miss Stoneman told on Lizzie, my father would have to let me marry you. I sent my grandmother to deliver letters to every village I know of."

"Yes... I met this grandmother of yours. She's rather odd, isn't she?" I say. Ahmir laughs.

"She is indeed, but we love her for it. She returned with the news that you rode with her in a stolen buggy, but she wouldn't give you the letter. She assured me you would come on the train, but I knew something was wrong when you didn't come in a couple of days."

"Yes, something was very wrong," I laughingly interrupt. "Your grandmother didn't fit into her calculations that I had no money."

"So she later realized. But now, you look so tired. Go to sleep; my father wants to meet you in the morning."

"Okay," I hear myself say. I give him a good, long kiss goodnight before he extinguishes the kerosene lamp and leaves the room.

It never felt better to sleep than it does tonight: my letter safely tucked inside a drawer and me tucked inside this warm, soft bed. My heart is at ease, and soon, I am asleep.

Eight

In the morning, Ahmir and I visit the king in a room I have never been in before. King Roe is wearing a cream-colored robe this time, not a red one.

"How are you, Your Royal Majesty?" I say with a curtsy. Ahmir bows to his father.

"Hello, my son. Hello, Miss Chapel," he greets us. "I am quite well, Miss Chapel, thank you. And yourself?"

"I am getting over being sick."

"Ah, illness is horrid. But we've already met, have we not, Miss Chapel?"

"Er- yes, in the halls once, I believe."

"I didn't know that," Ahmir pipes up.

"It was a brief meeting, let me assure you," mutters King Roe. "This fine young lady is an early riser."

"Yes, I grew up in a village," I laugh. I am surprised to find King Roe so much more polite than he was the first time we met.

"Father, as you can see, Edelweiss is the girl I want to marry."

"I gave my consent, didn't I? I don't see why I would withdraw it, not now, anyway. Let's eat breakfast." We all stand and walk to the dining hall, where we meet up with Maddie Jane and Maddie Grace.

"Father, why can't you eat with us more often?" Maddie Jane asks the king.

"Yes, Father, why? I like it when you eat with us," adds her sister. The king shakes his head.

"There is too much to be done, my girls. This is a special occasion. I am welcoming the newest member of the royal family." I smile as Ahmir lays his hand on mine.

"What does your father do?" Roe asks me. I glance at Ahmir, and he answers for me.

"He's an individualist soldier."

"Individualist?" Roe repeats. "You mean he's against the End Raiders." Ahmir nods. King Roe turns to me.

"Do you agree with your father's philosophy?" he demands.

"No," I assure him. "I disagree with my father in every way. It has been a long time since we have been a family."

"And how's your mother?" he asks. I have to think before replying because I don't know how my mother is. We have always had a decent relationship with each other, but with my father coming home, I haven't paid much attention to her wellbeing. She must be devastated to lose me. I feel terrible for her, but there's nothing I can do.

"She is undoubtedly upset at my running away, but she has my father. She will be okay."

After breakfast, King Roe leaves us, but he blesses our marriage, which is the important part. Once he goes, I address Ahmir.

"Your father seems so polite sometimes and rude at other times. Is he often like that?"

"My father has always been rather aggressive, but my mother's death has affected him in every way."

"People say Roe murdered her," I recall. "It must be horrible to suffer a tragedy and be blamed for it all at once."

"My father never admits to being sad. He is afraid of being portrayed as weak. That's why they say he murdered my mother. He was always being aggressive toward her. He saw it as a way to flaunt his toughness."

"And your mother didn't complain?"

"Never. Father would bully her for years, and she wouldn't say a word. My mother had a stiff upper lip, which was good for publicity but not good when it came to being with my father."

"That is cruel. Didn't he see what he was doing?"

"Yes," Ahmir says softly. "Right after she died, he saw."

The next three weeks flash by far too quickly. Wedding plans take up all hours of the day, and my time alone with Ahmir is limited. We have to steal a few quiet moments with each other, and that is always the highlight of my day.

Before I know it, my wedding has arrived, and I spend my last few hours as Edelweiss Chapel preparing for the ceremony. The maids paint my nails a lavender color to match the hue of the wedding cake and Ahmir's tie. I'm not allowed to see Ahmir all day, and I am so anxious about the wedding that I can't stop chewing my lip, even though this isn't a habit I've ever had.

My gown is the most gorgeous thing. It has loads of white fabric and a train draping three feet behind me. It has long translucent sleeves and reaches down to my white silk slippers. The maids apply make-up on me and do my hair. My veil is as long as my dress and has a pattern of edelweiss flowers. My tiara is silver with diamonds embedded in it. I feel like an expensive piece of jewelry myself.

A maid knocks on my door.

"Come in," I greet her. The maid curtseys.

"Your Highness, a letter has come in."

"From who?" My eyebrows raise.

"Mr. and Mrs. Chapel." I frown.

"I won't see it," I say, crossing my arms. "I don't want to be angry right before my wedding."

"Yes, miss," the maid answers and turns away. "Shall I keep it for you?" I hesitate before replying. Do I really want to read this letter? I decide that I do.

"Yes, that's fine," I answer. "I'll read it later." Another maid enters the room, her cheeks flushed.

"They're ready for you," she informs me. I hold my breath and stand as the two maids direct me out of the room.

The orchestra we hired plays the Wedding March, and I slowly make my way down the aisle. The wedding is in the church where King Roe married his wife, and Queen Lotus married King Leroy. Of course, Prince Ahmir looks magnificent as a lion from where he stands, waiting for me.

I stare into his shimmering green eyes, and he gazes into my plain hazel ones. We smile at each other, and Ahmir seems to be glowing with happiness. My knees tremble, and it seems ages until I am right in front of him, holding his hand. An officiator says many words I can't quite hear, but the important part is that I remember to say, "I do," exactly when I should. So does Ahmir, and finally, the officiator stops talking, and Ahmir and I kiss.

My name is Princess Edelweiss. I am royalty now. I twist my beautiful gold wedding ring around my finger. There is a huge party where we talk, dance, and eat cake. The guests all congratulate Ahmir and I, showering us with gifts. Newspaper writers and journalists interview us, asking us personal questions I don't know how to answer.

"When did you first realize that Ahmir loved you back?"

"When I first ate lunch with him," I answer, trying to be as honest as possible.

"Why did Ahmir almost marry Lizzie?"

"It was a mistake. His father wanted him to marry the daughter of an End Raider, but she wasn't."

"What was it like being a poor villager?" This one I have to think about. I know it was terrible, but what was it *like*?

"It's like being on a road and knowing you're supposed to go one way, but the signs are pointed in the other direction everywhere you look. Like you want to go somewhere, but there's a roadblock, and everyone tells you it's hopeless. It's like arriving somewhere, and everyone around you is content, but you're disappointed because it's all wrong."

"If you could say one thing to your parents, what would it be?"

"I'm happier than I've ever been, and if you love me, you'll be happy for me and not angry with me."

Next, they interview Ahmir.

"Were you concerned you wouldn't be able to marry Princess Edelweiss because of her position in society?"

"No," Ahmir answers. "I was sure my father would allow it, and I don't care at all whether she was poor or rich. She's rich now."

"How do you think your father is taking the marriage?"

"Very well. He's exceptionally fond of Edelweiss, and they get along just fine."

"Where do you plan on taking your honeymoon?"

"We're going to travel to all of the seven kingdoms and meet the rulers of their society."

"What value do you think Princess Edelweiss will add to the End Raiders?"

"Edelweiss's effects will go far past what anyone expects, including myself. I don't know what she will do because I cannot see the future, but I do know that her name will go down in history as something impactful."

When we finish our interview, I stand beside Ahmir.

"Are you happy to be married?" my husband asks.

"I'm just glad I'm here with you and not with Vashti Marlow." Ahmir smirks.

"I'd like to meet this Vashti person. Find out why he thinks he can take you from me." We laugh and kiss again.

After all the festivities, Ahmir and I prepare to leave on our honeymoon. We are going to travel the whole Realm over ten months, and we are taking a ship to all seven kingdoms. The crowds don't yet know me, so I am both excited and nervous to become a public image.

My dream has come true. Here I am, not just raised in society, but a princess. My true love is by my side, and I'm taking a world excursion. Life could not have worked out more perfectly, though I struggled immensely to get here.

"Let's say goodbye to the family," Ahmir suggests. We see the twins first.

"Goodbye, Maddie Grace, bye, Maddie Jane," I say, giving each of them a hug.

"Good luck," Maddie Jane replies. "I still can't see why I can't go too."

Ahmir and I laugh. Maddie Grace only cries because she will miss us, but we assure her we will be back soon.

"I *knew* I liked you," she tells me. I kiss Baby Livingston on the cheek. King Roe appears with his mother, Lotus.

"Farewell, my children," he says, giving us each a kiss on our forehead. The king takes my hand into his own.

"Take care of my son," he tells me in a voice more gentle than I've ever heard him speak.

"I will, Your Majesty," I promise. King Roe turns his attention to Ahmir.

"Goodbye, Ahmir."

"I'll see you in a few months," Ahmir assures him. Lotus winks at me.

"So you made it, eh, girl? I hope you don't get seasick; it's a horrible experience."

"Goodbye, Grandma, take care of yourself," Ahmir says.

"Ah, don't worry about me. You've got a whole Realm to convince you'll take care of all their problems, even though you won't."

"I'll try," Ahmir replies.

"I hate a central government," she mutters, shaking her head. Then she and her son leave with the little girls.

"We have a ship to catch," I tell Ahmir. He nods, and we take a carriage to the ocean. I have never seen the beach before, and it's strange to smell salt in the air, feel sand beneath my feet, and watch foamy waves crash against the rocks. The ship that awaits us is gigantic; it should fit a hundred people and not two. We board it together, celebrating a new chapter in our lives.

The first kingdom we will go to is Ginger Holmes. Next is Cap, and then Le Beth. After that, we will visit Chan Hinge, home of the End Raiders. Bridger and High Fire will be last, and then we'll return to Seth Sound. We will spend ten days in each kingdom.

The ship leaves the dock, and Ahmir and I are off on our long honeymoon. One of the servants shows us to the master bedroom. We will be given a tour of the ship tomorrow. The entire boat is so lavish and expensive-looking that I can't imagine how much money went into its making.

"When was this ship built?" I ask Ahmir in wonder once we're in our room.

"More than two hundred years ago."

"This whole place is amazing," I exclaim.

"Nothing will ever be as amazing as the fact that I am married to you, and we'll spend our whole lives beside each other." I smile and glow on my inside.

"My life starts today," I announce. "This whole honeymoon, let's pretend there never was anybody named Edelweiss Chapel. I was born as Princess Edelweiss, and I have always been married to you."

"Yes," Ahmir agrees. "And I have always been with you. In fact, we've been on this ship our whole lives, and we love it. We never want to leave it, and we won't as long as we live."

"Never?" I laugh.

"Never," he confirms.

"It sounds wonderful," I say. "And we never had parents. We've been on this ship since the invention of time."

"We saw the beginning of the world," adds Ahmir. We come up with a world all our own, fantastical and beautiful. We talk about it in bed together and see it in our dreams.

It is a new Realm, *our* Realm. Nobody can rupture our peace. Nothing wrong ever happens in our Realm, and disasters don't exist.

We even go as far as to say that we're the only people in the world. And we are because when I press my cheek against my husband's chest, I can't imagine why anyone else would need to be created.

Nine

In the days of our honeymoon, time seems to blend and in the days and weeks spent on our ship, I cannot recount. Only the seventy days spent on land can I remember clearly.

When we arrive at Ginger Holmes one evening, military soldiers greet and escort us to the castle, Portifa. We will stay with King Jacob, even though the king of Ginger Holmes dislikes End Raiders. Ahmir tells me that both Queen Lotus and her late husband, King Leroy, were excellent friends with King Jacob before Leroy was shot and killed.

Though we expect a butler, the king himself opens the door and smiles at us, holding out both hands. Ahmir and I shake one at the same time. I can't help but giggle as I try to figure out which hand to shake with.

"Welcome, End Raiders. And congratulations!"

"Thank you, King Jacob," Ahmir says, letting go of his hand.

"Eh, it's alright. Anything for the grandson of my old friends. I hope you're liking royal life, Edelweiss."

"Oh, yes, thank you, your majesty," I reply.

"Very well. Put your things away. I will show you to your room." The older man surprises me with how spry he is and leads us quickly to our room. It is quite as beautiful as Seth Sound's castle, though everything seems to involve artwork, whereas our castle back home is bare with its pure marble. Paintings, sculptures, pottery, and tapestries are all over Portifa Palace.

Our room is large and elaborate, decorated with gold and violet colors. Ahmir and I sleep well and don't wake up until very late. When we do, we get lost in the halls but eventually make it to the breakfast room.

Unlike our Dining Room in Seth Sound, the breakfast room has only one small table with an elaborate glass chandelier hanging directly above it. We eat crunchy bread with strange foods like salted fish and capers. After breakfast, we walk along the beach and collect shells. Ahmir spots a small crab, which I have never seen before, but Ahmir, Jacob, and I are all too scared to touch it.

Jacob wants to swim in the ocean, but Ahmir isn't a strong swimmer, and I can't swim at all, so we make a sandcastle instead. The king of Ginger Holmes is a bit quirky, but he is kind and fun. He teaches us how to make a blade of grass sound like a horn, which I get very good at. I'm amazed at the loud sound such a tiny blade of grass can make.

"How's Lotus doing?" he asks once.

"She's very well," I say.

"Ah, that's good," he replies, staring out the window. "I haven't seen her in many years."

"Maybe someday you'll come visit," Ahmir suggests. Jacob shakes his head.

"I wish I could, but Lotus is not the young woman she used to be. Leroy's death affected her deeply."

"What was she like when she was younger?" Ahmir asks. King Jacob chuckles.

"She was wild. You couldn't contain her. Lotus would do as Lotus pleased, and she made sure everyone knew it. She and I have been friends since we were children."

"What was my grandfather like?" Ahmir continues.

"I remember when Lotus met Leroy. It was at my mother's coronation. Leroy wasn't a bad fellow, but I was always surprised with the match. He was so serious; I could never imagine them together."

We avoid the subject of politics during our stay, as we don't want to offend our host. We don't give any speeches for the End Raiders in Ginger Holmes, though we make public appearances to wave to the crowds. Many people in Ginger Holmes distrust us but are excited to meet us anyway. Everyone wants a glimpse of the prince and princess no matter what side of the war they are on.

King Jacob lives by himself, with no family or friends. He must be very lonely. He tells us that he does not usually invite strangers into his home, but we are children, so he made an exception. I wonder what would have happened if Lotus had married Jacob instead of Leroy. King Leroy was not proactive about the End Raiders, though King Jacob is currently at war against them. They might not have killed Leroy, but Jacob may not have survived. Somehow, I think that Lotus married the wrong man.

I feel bad for Jacob, so I try to be entertaining and cheerful during our visit. Ahmir and I only like some of the food given to us, but he is more picky than I am. Ginger Holmes has a lot of seafood, and neither of us are accustomed to the slimy texture of almost everything. Everything tastes either salty or fishy, most things both.

"I could never live here," Ahmir tells me. "I wouldn't be able to eat."

"I'm sure you would get used to it," I say.

"I don't know. I'm not sure I could get used to eating salty goop all the time."

The weather is beautiful our entire stay, and we spend most of our time outdoors. One day, we picnic in King Jacob's favorite spot. It's a landscape of green grass and a huge banyan tree overlooking the sea. King Jacob stares at it, watching the waves crash into the rocks.

I turn to Ahmir and wrap my arms around him. He kisses me and lies on his back.

"Edelweiss," he says.

"Yes?"

"Have you thought about having children?" I hesitate before responding because I have always viewed children as an unnecessary expense rather than an heir to the throne.

"I suppose I have to," I reply.

"No, you don't have to, but it would undoubtedly be the preferred method."

"How else would the End Raiders have an heir?"

"My siblings could take the throne after me, and their children could continue the line, or we could adopt."

"I would rather have my own than adopt children," I tell him. "Though I would want them to have a good father."

"Am I not good?" Ahmir frowns.

"You will be busy like your father is now. Didn't you see how much your sisters wanted to spend time with Roe? I know how it is to have an absent parent in your life. I don't want my children to suffer the same way."

"Edelweiss, my father is extremely attentive to his children, and I will be as well."

"Your father?" I repeat in surprise. "He is hardly ever around your siblings. I would consider you more of their father than he is." Ahmir sits up now.

"How would you know what kind of a parent my father is? You've only just met him, and I've known him my whole life. At some point, I have to balance my personal life with my responsibilities."

"If I'm going to have kids, I want them to be your priority, Ahmir. A child only gets two parents; I will not have that compromised to fit your agenda."

"My agenda? Would I rather be working than spending time with you and my family? I do everything for the good of the Realm, not for my pleasures."

"We haven't even started a family yet, and you're already overshadowing our needs for everyone else's."

"People need me, Edelweiss, and I'm shocked that you don't support my ambitions to help others as much as possible. If that means sacrificing some time for myself, so be it. Saving lives is much more important."

King Jacob suddenly turns to us.

"Are you two arguing already? You've only just been married." Horrified, I realize he's right.

"I'm sorry, Ahmir," I tell my husband. "I'm just trying to do what's right for the family."

"And I'm just trying to do what's right for the Realm," Ahmir responds, still bitter. "But I think we can drop it for now, okay?"

I agree, and we don't pick up the subject again. King Jacob still looks alarmed.

"Never fight with your spouse, my children. You don't want anything to go unsaid if something happens to them." Ahmir puts a hand on my shoulder.

"Don't worry, Edelweiss," he tells me. "Nothing's going to happen to either one of us." Jacob raises his eyebrows but doesn't say anything. I put my argument with Ahmir out of my mind and think about what a beautiful day it is.

Ten

When our time is up at Ginger Holmes, we say goodbye to King Jacob.

"Thanks for letting us stay," Ahmir tells him.

"No problem, my boy," he replies, smiling at us both.

"Take care," I say.

"Take care of Lotus."

"We will," Ahmir promises, and we're on our way to Cap, the land of philosophy. Politics run high there, but not much violence goes around. Most people there do more thinking and speaking than doing.

Our weeks at sea are enjoyable. Ahmir and I are the only passengers besides the huge crew waiting on us. We have the whole place to ourselves and can do whatever we wish. Time goes at a different pace when we're floating on the ocean, and soon enough, we are docked at the kingdom of Cap.

Cap has a king, but it is the only kingdom that is primarily a democracy. The king doesn't do much in the way of decision making and his power is limited. This is preferable among the people who live in Cap, as they don't like power-hungry rulers, which makes almost all of them against the End Raiders. In order to rule all of the Realm, the End Raiders must find favor among the people of Cap. We can trust that there won't be much violent opposition here, but we have bodyguards just in case. Most of the people are curious about us and will hear the speeches we are to give.

The king, unlike Jacob, does not welcome us into his home. His name is King Prongley DeSalvo. We get a unique cottage, which is comfortable and spacious enough for the two of us, but I can tell that the king is not too eager to invite us into his land.

King Prongley gave us permission to speak from the balcony of one of his ancient palaces, Buckingham, and Ahmir is practicing his lines.

"I don't see why you're rehearsing so much; we'll have our scripts," I tell him.

"I know, but what if I mess up? This may be our only chance to recruit Cap to the End Raiders."

"Oh, it'll be fine," I assure him.

When it is time to deliver our speech, Ahmir and I walk hand in hand to the palace, where many people crowd around. When we come onto the balcony, everybody gives us their full attention, but nobody cheers. I can detect skepticism in most people's faces, and I'm determined to help the image of the End Raiders, for my father-in-law, but also for my husband because I know Ahmir will one day be king and the leader of the End Raiders.

"Good morning," Ahmir greets the population. "I am Prince Ahmir from the land of Seth Sound, my home country."

"My name is Princess Edelweiss, and I recently married Ahmir," I shout so everyone can hear me.

"Our goal is to inform you of the principles the End Raiders hold most dear. One of them is unity. Unity is what brings us together. Unity is why I am here today. I am from Seth Sound, which is foreign, but you, the people of Cap, have still welcomed my wife and me into your kingdom. When the End Raiders have control, we will not be foreign to one another. We will be from the same kingdom, the Realm. All of our brothers and sisters will be from the Realm, and nothing more will divide us politically."

"Unity is one," I hear my voice say. I look down at my script because I forget my next words. "Another is loyalty. You are all loyal to your people and to your government. Let it be so when the End Raiders are your government. Have faith in your leaders and Realm; you will never wish for a different government. But battle against us, and the world will become chaos. We must band together and be loyal to one another so that this is not so. So that our sons and daughters, our posterity, can live peacefully." Ahmir picks up his lines.

"Peace is why we are here today. We are peaceful people, all of us. Some of you may doubt this. Some of you may say my father is not peaceful. There have been rumors that my father murdered my mother. Gossip no more. This is false. My father believes in a land that knows no violence but only absolute freedom."

"Freedom," I echo. "Before I met my dear prince, my father arranged my marriage to a man named Vashti Marlow, in which I had no say in our union. This is not the way the End Raiders wish you to follow us. We will never force you to unite with us. We will never force you to become one, but we will hope and persevere until you give up your fight and come willingly to us."

"Perseverance," booms Ahmir's strong voice. "The End Raiders will never quit, neither on you nor our principles. We will stay true until the end of time, which is why they are called the End Raiders. They will be here and never die away until they have finished their job. The never-ending job. The work of humankind to strive on until the end."

"And so," I conclude. "We will not say 'the end.' We will say 'until the end.' Thank you for your time this morning."

"Until the end," Ahmir closes. When we finish, about half of the people clap, which is fantastic, seeing the improvement we've made since the beginning of our speech.

"How were we?" I ask Ahmir.

"Very good, Edelweiss, very good. But tell me, do you believe it? Or do you still follow your father's ideas?" I hesitate before I reply.

"I don't care. I have never cared about politics, so I just go along with it, you know?" Ahmir nods.

"I see. Well, you sounded very convincing."

"Good. Whatever helps you helps me, darling." We get a lot of attention from the people and give a couple more speeches during our stay. Ahmir and I go to a store and we buy a newspaper. It would be hard to miss the bold caption on the front of the paper:

Seth Sound Prince and His New Wife Speak for the End Raiders at Buckingham Palace

The young Prince Ahmir (18) and his new wife, Princess Edelweiss (16), go on their honeymoon to Cap, where they give a now-famous speech titled 'Until The End.' Princess Edelweiss's father speaks on the topic.

"My daughter is deranged. I have been fighting against the End Raiders for eight years, and she has always agreed with me. Suddenly, she mysteriously disappears while working at the castle, leaving only a small letter behind. She returned a few days later looking a little strange, and she had a temperamental fit right before running out of the house and never coming back. A few weeks later, she's married to the prince. Something dodgy is going on. My daughter would never do this on her own.'"

Nobody has heard Princess Edelweiss's thoughts on the matter yet. She has proclaimed her full support to the End Raiders, and we have no evidence yet to support Mr Chapel's theory that she has somehow been manipulated by the prince or the king.

I look up at Ahmir.

"This isn't good. My father is speaking against us," I say. Ahmir reads the newspaper and smiles.

"But we made it to the front cover, right? Publicity is good, and on the backside, they included the transcript for our speech."

"I'm worried," I say. "What is going to happen with my father?" Ahmir shakes his head.

"I'm hoping he'll be perceived as just an angry parent. There *is* no truth to what he's saying, so let's not worry about it, okay?"

"Alright," I agree. The rest of the day is relaxing, though I don't heed Ahmir's advice. I worry about my father all the time, not entirely *about* him, but what damage his words will do. I have to make a speech to tell the world what he says is false. But if my father can make a stand on the front page of a national newspaper, who else can? What will they say? I just don't want anyone to hurt Ahmir.

I don't know how well I like the End Raiders, but I was honest when I told Ahmir I don't care because nothing like that can matter anymore, not when Ahmir is the only one I care about. As long as other people agree with the End Raiders and Ahmir leads them, it's good for me.

I know that one day, when Roe dies or otherwise abdicates, Ahmir and I will rule Seth Sound and the End Raider empire. He will take his father's position as the Raiders' King, and I will be the Raiders' Queen.

I try not to think so far into the future, but my whole life seems to revolve around this honeymoon. In our last few days in Cap, I give my first speech on my own. The king permits me to return to Buckingham Palace and I deliver an unscripted speech to the people of Cap.

"Thank you for welcoming me back. A few days ago, my husband and I gave a speech to bring to light the principles of the End Raiders. As you know, my father responded to this with accusations toward my husband and my new family. I believe I am the only person who can honestly tell you all how false his words are. My father is angry, and he is hurt because he lost a daughter. But the reason he lost his daughter was not because I have been brainwashed, but because I stood up, and I took to heart the values of the End Raiders.

"My childhood was not a fortunate one. I was poor, and my father abandoned my mother and me to fight against the End Raiders in war. He left his own family for violence and murder. He cannot let go of the old ways, as we all must do. In order to make room for innovative and better ways, we all must release our divided kingdoms. It is not a lack of loyalty that will drive you to do so because you will be one nation. You will be the Realm. Not the Seven Kingdoms of the Realm. Not Cap inside of the Realm. But the one Realm that has always been and always will be until the end.

"My father says I have been manipulated, and I have, but by his hand, not the End Raiders'. He has tried to make me marry a man I did not wish to. Where is my freedom? My father had no loyalty to his family, in which he forsook. My father had no faith in me to make my own decisions. My father fought in war instead of making peace. He doesn't stand for unity but for separation. He opposes the royal family. He is not faithful to his country. It is people like my father who hold back the End Raiders. Do not let it be you. I did not and will not let it be me. Thank you." This time, almost everyone claps for me when I finish. I hurry back from the balcony to where Ahmir is waiting.

"When did you write that speech?" Ahmir asks.

"I didn't," I reply. "I just made it up." Ahmir's eyebrows raise.

"That was amazing, Edelweiss, really. Especially someone who doesn't even care about the End Raiders."

"But I care about you," I say. "And I delivered that speech for you because I know it is the only way to gain the people's trust."

"Thank you," he tells me. "It worked." I know he is telling the truth because of the crowd's reaction.

On the last day in Cap, Ahmir and I say goodbye to the people of Cap, and we pack our things. King Prongley pays our cottage a visit before we go.

"Hello?" I answer the door when he knocks. I recognize him as the king right away. "How are you, sir?"

"I'm fine, thank you. May I sit?"

"Of course," I say, leading him in. Ahmir sits at the Dining Room table.

"Is there something we can do for you, your majesty?" Ahmir asks him.

"Yes, I would like to speak to your father about working with him on this project. I have always been curious about the End Raiders, and now it seems the right choice is to let it go through. Cap needs to stay out of war, you see."

"Violence should always be avoided," Ahmir agrees. "My father would be delighted to hear this news." King Prongley nods again.

"I thought as much," he says. "How can I contact him? I never talk to the kings of other lands." I leave the room to finish packing, and the two talk for another hour. When Ahmir is finished, he joins me.

"The news could not be more splendid, Edelweiss. Once the other kingdoms see that the Land of Philosophy has done this, everyone else will, too."

"I bet your father will be especially pleased."

"For sure, I think he will be proud."

"Who could help to be proud of you, Ahmir? After all that you've done for people."

"Thank you, Edel. I will write to my father right now. Oh, he'll be so happy!"

"Yes, but I can't say the same for my father."

"Don't worry about your father. We'll leave Cap today and head to Ginger Holmes. Your father won't ever see you again."

"I hope so," I say as we head to the ship.

Eleven

Leaving Cap is easier than leaving Ginger Holmes because we made no new friends here. However, our mission is undoubtedly successful because the End Raiders now hold three of the seven kingdoms: Seth Sound, Chan Hinge, and Cap. Chan Hinge is the headquarters for the End Raiders.

I can tell that winter is beginning because little flakes of snow fall from the sky and frost can be found on the ship. The closer we get to Le Beth, the colder it gets. Le Beth used to be known as Antarctica, which means "opposite the bear," but I think both names miss the point. It should be called Ice, Snow, or Cold Wind. That is all Le Beth is made of, as Ahmir and I discover when we step off our ship and a blizzard rages outside.

We packed for all kinds of weather because we'll be seeing all of the seasons, and it's a good thing we did. Men with lanterns trudge to our ship and hand Ahmir and me a rope so we don't stray from the light bearers. It is impossible to see anything except a faint glow from a lantern that seems to be a mile off but is really a foot from my face. I can't see anybody, but I hear Ahmir shout above the howling wind. I try to yell back, to assure him that I'm still here and alright, but the gush of cold air catches my voice, and the cutting blades of snow and ice pierce my mouth and singe my throat.

The cold is more painful and acute than anything I've ever experienced. It seems to sizzle in some areas, burning my arms, face, and neck with its sharp tongues even though I am wearing a scarf and my coat sleeves are long. In other places, like my feet and fingers, the pain numbs all feelings except the deadened lick of frostbite.

We are heading to the castle, where we will stay. How can anybody live in conditions like these? Ahmir calls to me again, but the blood on my lips seems to have frozen, and I cannot cry out as I try to do. The light-bearers stop briefly, and I run into one from behind. They are turning a large metal wheel, and I can barely make out a gate opening. We go through, and instantly, the wind is still. I hear a ringing in my ears; the silence is so sharp but calming. My whole body is still frigid, but at least we are inside.

The building around me is bare, made of bricks on all sides, even the roof. The light-bearers keep walking, and I numbly reach Ahmir, who stands ten feet in front of me. He grasps at my mitten-encased hand.

"I thought I lost you," he gasps, trying to get a deep breath.

"I'm so cold," I say faintly. Ahmir puts an arm around me, and we follow the light bearers as they take us inside the castle, which seems fully enclosed in a brick dome. Inside, there are roaring fires every-where. Maids stroll into the room and unwrap the garments we have on. Snow piles on the floor as layer after layer is taken off. I am so stiff, I can't help her, even though I want to. One maid pulls me to a couch next to one of the fires.

I doubt if I'll ever be warm again. My feet feel stiff and numb. They are ghostly white but glint slightly blue and unnaturally shiny in the firelight. The maid sits at my feet and begins to do something with her hands on them that makes them burn; I would have said she is jabbing pins and needles into me if I hadn't been able to see her empty hands moving.

Another maid serves me hot tea, which I spill down my face and scalds my skin. Fortunately, though, it warms my lips enough to speak normally again.

"Ahmir?" I shout. I hear somebody stand and move in my direction. Ahmir sits on the edge of the couch with his back to the fire. He gazes at me with concern. "Are you frostbitten?"

"I don't know," I whisper. I am ordered to stay on the couch until morning when a doctor can look at me. I've never had a doctor check me out before, and I'm nervous about it.

I sleep alone on the slim couch tonight, watching the flames flicker strangely. If I listen hard, I can still hear the wild whistling outside. My whole body aches and sharp pains shoot through me whenever I move.

The following day, a doctor comes to look at me. He is a very short, grave man with a handlebar mustache. He does lots of painful little experiments on me, which make me cry out occasionally.

"Kindly lift your foot up for me while I use this little hammer to tap it," he says.

"Kindly tell me if you can feel this." I answer him with a sound between a groan and a whimper.

"Would you kindly smile?" I move my cheeks weakly, but it hurts too bad to continue.

"Thank you kindly, my dear." His way of saying these things is irritating and ironic because his saying "kindly" makes me more hostile.

When the doctor has diagnosed me with mild frostbite on my fingers, toes, cheek, and right ear, he gives me a serum to apply and leaves. Ahmir and I discuss our plans for the next ten days while he helps me spread the serum.

"The queen and king aren't here right now," he informs me. "I was speaking to the princess earlier. She and her brother are the only royalty home, and she says that the blizzards aren't likely to stop in the next week or two and that we'll probably be stuck indoors the whole time."

"How do people even stand this?" I ask miserably.

"The prince says that the brick dome serves as their outdoors, so they don't really get sunlight unless the storm calms for a time."

"Ugh, but it will be so dark and cold," I complain. "You can't play when you can't even see each other."

"Yes, that's what I was thinking too, but the prince assured me that you can see just fine with lanterns. Of course, the doctor says you should not leave this couch for another three days."

"Three days!" I exclaim incredulously. "I've never been bedbound, but I've always been somewhat afraid of it." Ahmir doesn't have time to reply because, at that moment, the prince and princess walk into the room.

"Hello, Princess Edelweiss," the prince of Le Beth greets me. "I hope you get better soon."

"Yes," his sister giggles. "Because we were thinking of having a ball while you are here, but you can't dance in bed, can you?"

"No, I suppose you can't," I say. "Pardon me, but what are your names?"

"I'm Kurt," the boy answers. "This is my older sister, Rose."

"How do you do?" Rose chortles.

"Not quite well at the moment," I reply grimly, glancing at my swollen hands.

Princess Rose looks about my age, perhaps slightly younger than me. She has short, blond, curly hair that falls in ringlets around her face and dangles somewhat above her shoulders. Her cheeks are very pink, and she is a tall, slim girl. Her skin is almost paper white and a little transparent; her blue eyes are pale and milky. She has a high-pitched voice, a bubbly laugh, and a dimpled smile.

Prince Kurt is about thirteen, with small, solemn gray eyes and fine, dusty blond hair. He has sharp, well-chiseled features: a narrow nose and a prominent chin. His forehead is small, and his neck is long. Like his sister, he is slim and tall. He talks politely and mechanically, an important feature of public royal life. His emotions run on the inside, beneath those earnest eyes, and are not mirrored onto his face or exhibited in his words or actions. He doesn't even seem to have much personality.

The three days when I am bed bound are agony. I lay on the couch all day and night, sometimes with Rose reading a book to me or just talking. Ahmir stays close by me most of the time, though the Le Beth royalty often disappears for hours.

On the last day of my sentence, Rose comes into the room with the doctor. She talks the whole time about dancing and dresses. Princess Rose is determined to host an honorary ball for Ahmir and me. She can't wait for all her little friends to see us.

"They'll just love you. I *know* they will, Princess Edelweiss. My friends are some of the nicest people in the whole Realm."

The doctor finishes checking me out with a satisfied smile on his face. "I can see you have been using that serum. It has made quite a difference for you. You don't have to stay on the couch anymore."

"Oh good," I cry. "Ahmir will be happy to hear that. I think he's tired of me just lying here, groaning." I spring up immediately but regret it. Pain shoots through me. Rose titters.

"Easy there, now. Don't get too excited." The doctor nods.

"Princess Rose is right. Take it slowly." I thank the doctor for his time and care, but Rose pays him.

"You're our guest," she says simply when I offer to pay her back. "You've been such a great patient and a good friend. I knew I could trust you as soon as I saw your speech in the newspaper."

I gasp, smiling at Ahmir delightedly.

"But that was all the way in Cap! People in Le Beth heard about it, too?"

"Oh yeah. News travels quickly, alright. Oh, here comes my brother." Prince Kurt, covered in snow, bows slightly.

"Excuse me, ma'am, I was wondering if you'd like to see outside." My heart leaps but then sinks again.

"I think you can hardly call that dirt dome outside, but alright."

"No, ma'am," he clarifies. "The blizzard stopped; we have a day of calm. Come outside. There's eight feet of snow out there." Rose lets out a squeal of excitement.

"Yes, Princess Edelweiss, you'll like it out there. It's so much fun when we can play outside in the snow. And so much of it! Do say you'll go, please?"

"Alright, I'll go, but where's Ahmir?"

"He's already out there, making snowballs," Kurt replies. Rose and I follow him outside, but Rose can't stand to walk and begins to skip. I remember to dress in many warm layers, so I don't have enough flexibility to do the same.

The temperatures outside are cold, of course, but the only surface of skin that the ice can touch is my nose and cheeks, which are still raw from my last venture in the outdoors of Le Beth. Ahmir waves us over to him, where he has begun to make a snowman. I bend down to help him, and soon, we have three giant snowballs on top of each other.

When Rose sees it, she gasps and tells us she has the best idea. When she comes back, she has two sticks and a carrot in her arms.

Rose pulls out two buttons from her pocket, and soon, we have a real snowman with sticks for arms, a carrot for a nose, and two buttons for eyes.

"What's his name?" Rose asks.

"Her name," Kurt corrects. "She's Everleigh."

"Why?" I ask. He replies by reciting a poem:

When finally the cold skies were clear,
I was looking all over for my dear
Everleigh.

I searched in all her favorite places,
But alas, I couldn't find any traces
Of Everleigh.

I thought of somewhere else to be,
Straining my eyes around to see
Everleigh.

Under the ice's shivery hold,
I found her body lying ice cold,
Dear Everleigh.

When she froze, her eyes did gloss,
How will I bear the terrible loss
Without Everleigh?

Kurt gives no further explanation of why he would name a snowman after a tragic poem and changes subjects.

"I remember when the snow covered the rooftops of every building around, and everyone was trapped in their houses."

"Was everyone okay? Did they have enough food?"

"Yes, everyone is prepared for being snowed in. It comes with the territory here."

The conversation continues, but I continue to dwell on Prince Kurt's poem. What if something happens to *my* love, just like the narrator's Everleigh and Lotus's Leroy. My fists clench and sweat despite the cold, and as I stare out into the white, bleak distance of Le Beth, I see in my mind horrors that could be waiting ahead.

We make tiny snowballs and hit each other with them, but then it gets cold and we're all tired. We go back inside and allow our hands to melt by the fire.

"I wish we could be doing something for the End Raiders," sighs Ahmir.

"There's not a chance in this weather," Kurt points out. "And besides, people here aren't like the people in Cap. We're not about philosophy or thinking. We're cold, and we've always been cold. You'll die if you try to speak here."

There's a ringing silence after he says this, in which everyone absorbs the meaning of his words. My thoughts run backward, back to the prospect that was introduced by the recitation of Everleigh.

Rose gives a little sigh. "I wish we lived in Cap. I hate all the cold here and all the terrible tempers. I want a warm sun and thoughtful neighbors. I want a king as agreeable as King Prongley."

"That's hard to come by," I say. "King Prongley is very noble." Rose sighs again, this time slightly louder, and then she frowns.

"Yes," she agrees, though I'm not sure she's talking about what I had said, more likely some fanciful thought in her head. "Yes, I *would* like to live in Cap."

The wind begins to pick up again, and soon, a snowstorm rolls in. The rest of our stay is blizzardy, and there's not much that we do besides warm up at the fire, talk, and listen to Rose read tales of fire-breathing dragons, hoards of gold, and little creatures with hairy feet.

It's a book called The Hobbit by a man named JRR Tolkien, who lived centuries and centuries before the End Raiders ever existed, back when imagination was valued and people dreamed of such beautiful things. I begin to think of Tolkien as an old friend, waiting to share the secret of politics and government, which seems to be the thread this world holds on to.

Rose loves it dearly, and she says that once there were more books that Tolkien wrote, but they were destroyed in the End Raider's fires. When she says this, Ahmir looks uncomfortable because we all know that it was his ancestors who started those fires, his ancestors who smothered creativity.

Ahmir could never do such a thing, no matter what his relatives did. Ahmir will always be true to his word, and in the speech he and I gave, we promised against violence. I refuse to believe that he would go back on that oath.

When it is finally time for Ahmir and me to leave Le Beth, we thank Rose and Kurt, who did their best to entertain us in their drab kingdom.

"Goodbye," Kurt repeats. "My sister and I wish you safety and comfort for the rest of your trip."

"Thank you," I say.

"You are both welcome back any time," Rose adds. "You have brightened my days so much." I doubt that any circumstance could dampen her spirits for long. Even in the princess's most wistful moods, she bounces back to her giggles.

"Goodbye, Rose. Goodbye, Kurt," Ahmir waves. I can barely make out the children waving back to us because we are back in a blizzard, not half so bad as the one we came in with, but still violent. This time, Ahmir and I don't let go of each other and make it back safely to the ship. We are not sorry to leave Le Beth because the weather is tremendously terrible.

Twelve

Chan Hinge has always been associated with the End Raiders and, over the ages, has been home to the empire. A couple centuries ago, Chan Hinge was mostly abandoned, except by some homeless Raiders. Slowly, more people started to form an army. Now, Chan Hinge is the headquarters of the End Raiders. You're not allowed in the kingdom if you're not an End Raider.

The kind of speeches Ahmir is preparing for us to give are different from the ones we performed in Cap. At Chan Hinge, everyone knows the End Raider principles; they just need to be rallied. I won't be speaking, but I'll be standing with Ahmir.

When our ship docks at a seaport, Ahmir and I get off, but we're immediately waylaid by a crowd of Raiders.

"Your Highnesses," they yell. Some bow, others shout, "Until the End!" All of them invite us into their houses. They hold their hands to us and push signs into the air. I expect the End Raiders to be soldiers ready for battle, but they are poor, chaotic people: barefoot, unkept, and dirty.

Ahmir takes my hand and tells me to find children. When I spot two grimy toddlers sucking on their fingers, I wave him over. We ask the children where their parents are, and they point to a woman standing separately in the crowd with a baby in her arms. Ahmir comes over to where she stands and asks,

"Can my wife and I stay in your home while we are here?" She nods, though her face is unenthusiastic. The rest of the people all beg for

Ahmir to change his mind and stay with them, but Ahmir shakes his head at them.

"Come," the woman with the baby says, though I'm unsure if she's talking to us or her toddlers. All four of us follow her down a dusty street, similar to the one in the village that goes from my old home to town.

We follow the woman to her house, which is more like a shack. She opens the door and allows us to walk through.

"Ma?" a little boy's voice calls.

"I'm home, Terrance. We have company." There is only one room in this shack. Along the wall is a fireplace where stew cooks in a pot. In one corner, a tub of water sits. Four mats and one makeshift wooden crib are spread out in another corner. One of the mats is occupied by a gaunt boy.

"Who is it?" the boy asks through ashen lips.

"It's the prince and princess from Seth Sound. They have come to deliver us from poverty. That's what they tell us, anyway." Ahmir bites his lip.

"We'll try, ma'am," he assures her. The woman snorts.

"Don't try for me; I don't want your help. If you wanna save your skin, you better try for them."

"Who's them?" I ask.

"The Raiders. They're sick and tired of this life. They want your money. They want your power. They want your handouts. Believe me when I say they will do anything to get their miserable little fingers on ya." I suck in my breath. Ahmir stares at the little boy on the mat, who looks no more than ten.

"That's my boy over there," the woman says, following Ahmir's gaze. "Yeah? You think it's funny? Do you royals think it's funny he's dying? Probably won't make it past the spring; he won't." I can't believe the woman is saying this in front of her son, but the little boy doesn't flinch.

"That's horrible," Ahmir says. "What's wrong with him?" The woman cackles obnoxiously.

"What's wrong with him? I'll tell you what's wrong with him. He's hungry, that's what. And he's crippled." She picks up a wooden spoon and stirs the stew. I haven't eaten in a while, but I don't dare ask for any after what I've just heard. She puts some in a bowl and gives it to the toddlers. One of the toddlers is a scrawny boy who's probably three. The other is a bony girl of four or five. They both look like they haven't had a bath in a month, and the girl's hair is so matted and damaged I doubt it will ever repair.

The baby begins to scream, but the woman only hushes it and sets it down next to the crippled boy. Next, she puts a bowl of stew before her son and scrapes up the rest for herself. I feel very out of place in my pretty pink dress and perfectly done hair. I'm even wearing a necklace today, and now I feel terrible for all of it.

"May we sit?" Ahmir asks the woman, gesturing to the floor.

"Yes," the woman says tartly, and Ahmir and I sit on the dirty floor.

"I need to get on this woman's friendly side," Ahmir whispers. "I have so many questions for her. I just need her to talk."

"Excuse me, ma'am," Ahmir says as the woman sits down. "Can you tell us your name?" The woman looks somewhat surprised.

"Naila, Naila Brown."

"Thank you, Naila. Would you care to introduce me to your children?" he asks pleasantly.

"The baby is Walter. He's not mine. He's my nephew. My sister died giving birth, so I took him in."

"I'm sorry to hear about your sister," Ahmir says gravely. "The baby is so young; it must not have been more than a year ago."

"Nine months," Naila informs him.

"And are the others yours?"

"Yes, Milee over there is my only girl. She's seven years old now." I raise my eyebrows. Such a small girl can not possibly be seven. Does she ever get fed? "The other one is Clarence," Naila continues. "He's four and the quietest. Then, of course, there's Terrance. He's almost twelve, but I doubt he'll see his birthday. He was crippled at birth, and nothing will keep him alive."

"I'm so sorry," Ahmir interjects.

"Don't be. Nobody asked for your pity. A lot of people ask daily for your help, but not me. I don't need fancy skins giving me charity. Never have, never will. I don't need anyone's help. I made my kids; I'll keep my kids; they don't need anything else." The woman pauses and glances at the baby, Walter, who has started to fuss again. "I don't know why people think you're their fairy godmother, but to them, you are. So if you still want an army, you better live up to it." Ahmir nods.

"We will speak to them in the morning. Thank you for your hospitality, Naila. Where can we sleep?"

"Right where you're sitting. Unless you want to go outside." It's not as bad for me as it is for Ahmir. I'm used to sleeping on thin mats on a hard floor, whereas Ahmir has grown up on soft beds and plump mattresses. He groans all night, tossing and turning every few minutes. Despite this, however, I drift off just fine.

Early in the morning, I wake Ahmir up because Naila is still sleeping, and I want to stay out of her hair during the day and only come back at night to sleep.

"Ahmir." I shake him. "Let's get up and go to the market."

"Market? Market? Who would need- I don't want to- what market?" He sits up and rubs his face. "Why do we have to go so early?"

"To get away from Naila, obviously." Ahmir groans, rubbing his eyes again.

"Does it really have to be this early?"

"Come on, let's get out of this place."

"Let's wait for breakfast," Ahmir suggests.

"She's not going to feed us. I brought some money off of the ship. We'll buy breakfast there."

"What about getting answers from Naila?"

"What answers do you want, Ahmir? She already told us everything we need to know. We have to face the people now."

"Fine, but shouldn't we buy Naila breakfast too?"

"No, she doesn't want our help."

"But we have to help her, Edel. It's our job."

"She doesn't want it. Isn't that enough for you? Sometimes, people don't want your assistance."

"That's stupid," Ahmir scoffs. "Let's buy her some eggs or something."

"How about we leave the woman alone."

"How about we feed these poor children." I hear Terrence shift positions, and I glance at him.

"Do you really think he'll die?" I ask.

"He will if we don't save him."

"It's not our problem," I remind him. "There's nothing anyone can do. Naila told us that."

"Naila's been wrong before."

"Why do you want to help them so badly? We can help the rest of these people. Why did we even choose the Browns to stay with?"

"I can't believe you, Edelweiss. I thought you would want to help."

"I thought you would want to respect Naila's wishes."

"It's not her wish. It's a coverup. She *needs* our help."

"Who does?" a voice interjects. Ahmir and I turn to face Terrance, fully awake.

"No one," Ahmir deflects. "We're going to the market."

"Can I come with you?" I look at Ahmir, and I know we have the same thought in our heads: *How is a crippled boy going to go to the market with us?*

"I mean, can you?" I ask gingerly, afraid I might be insulting him.

"If you don't mind going slowly," he replies. "I use crutches, and it works pretty well, actually. I've always dreamed of having a wheelchair, the kind they have at those fancy hospitals, but they're too expensive, of course." I don't know what to say, so Ahmir fills in for me.

"Yeah, you can come. We're slow walkers anyway." We go to town together, very slowly, while Terrance tells us about life in Chan Hinge.

"Everyone loves you guys. You're like celebrities, but they expect you to come and rescue them, like superheroes, you know? My ma doesn't like that. She says we were meant to care for ourselves and our family, not worry about other people. She says I'm never to give or accept charity."

"Isn't that a little selfish?" I ask.

"She said it isn't because we're not taking any help."

"What happened to your father?" I ask unexpectedly. I hadn't meant to ask it, and now the question hangs in the air.

"I don't know who my father is," Terrance says simply. "Ma never talks about him."

"Are Clarence and Milee your half-siblings?" I puzzle.

"Yes, their father is this shepherd who lives a long way away," replies Terrance. "Ma doesn't like him anymore; she says he's a thief and a scoundrel. Can we stop for a moment to rest? My legs are tired. I usually don't walk this far." I glance at Ahmir in frustration. We're not even close to finding a store of any kind.

"Will your mother worry if she wakes up and you're gone?" Ahmir asks suddenly. Terrance considers this.

"Ma never wakes up this early; she sleeps in." I look at the sun and estimate it is probably six thirty already. "Alright," he says. "I've rested enough now. Let's keep walking." We walk for a long time while talking a little about Chan Hinge's poverty and take three more rest breaks before we get to a marketplace.

We buy lots of food, but we are so often stopped by a desperate person begging for money we soon run out. Ahmir goes to the ship to get more because it's far quicker than dragging Terrance along with us, and I have to turn down handouts to at least ten different people.

We buy the rest of our groceries and give more people charity. Ahmir and I decide that now is the best time to give a speech, but since there's no stage or castle balcony to do it on, we just speak to the large crowd by shouting.

"Dear End Raiders, citizens of Chan Hinge," Ahmir begins as the crowd hushes. "Last night, my wife and I arrived at these shores for our honeymoon, but not only that. We are here to check on our people." Ahmir is no longer reading from the script he wrote last week. He is altering it based on what we have been told by Naila and Terrance.

"It may be that we End Raiders have to suffer some. Grit, deter-mination, perseverance, resiliency. These traits don't come from easy times. They don't come from lavish lives. They come from hard work, effort, trials, hardships, and struggles. That is what builds our nation. We strive to work until the end, no matter what.

"We don't stop because we don't feel like going on. We aren't quitters. We are survivors, we are fighters, we are warriors, and we are Raiders. We have to show them what we're made of; we have to show them what we can do. Can we build the dream, Raiders? Because if you're with me, a Raider, you fight until the end. You struggle until the end. You conquer until the end. We're not built by fear; we're built by pain. And we take it until the last drop of our enemy's blood is on our tongues, and we can taste the victory."

For some reason, Ahmir's language scares me. It doesn't sound at all like what he told the people of Cap. He is with the other End Raider leaders, constantly manipulating, always twisting things, and permanently changing the truth. I wonder how much I trust the End Raiders, and right now, not at all. But I remember how I only want the Raiders to be successful, not because I agree with them, but because I stand with Ahmir.

No matter why he stands for the Raiders, or anyone else does, I stand with them because I love my husband.

"So, End Raiders, do we fight, or do we fade? Do we conquer, or do we compromise? Do we defeat, or do we die? I ask you this today because today is not the day to quit. Today is not the day to give in. Today is the day to dare, restore hope, and resume our struggle... until the end." This speech is met with cheers, yells, and stomping. They believe him, and they will listen to him.

Ahmir takes my hand and leads me through the crowds. Terrance hobbles toward us with his crutches.

"You're such an amazing speaker!" he compliments Ahmir. "Maybe I'll be an End Raider one day too."

"Undoubtedly, you will be," Ahmir replies.

"Even with my leg?" he asks.

"Even with your leg," Ahmir assures Terrance. "There's a need for all positions in war, not just combat." They talk about this the whole way back to his mother's house, but I don't listen much.

When we arrive back, we are met by a furious Naila.

"Where were you?" she shouts at us. "Why did you take my son?"

"We went to the marketplace, Ma," Terrance pleads. "We didn't mean to scare you. I thought you'd still be asleep."

"I would be if Walter hadn't started howling and you three were gone," she scolds.

"I'm sorry, ma'am," I apologize. "We didn't mean to frighten you."

"Humph, well, don't do it again, or I'll think you've kidnapped the boy." Unfortunately for Ahmir and me, Naila doesn't get any friendlier the following week. Terrance isn't allowed to come with us to the marketplace anymore, dramatically increasing our speed, and Ahmir continues to do daily speeches. Each one gets more intense and violent, but the people love it. They stop begging for money, and the crowds get larger and larger.

Many Raiders offer for us to stay in their homes, but we only stay with the Browns.

"I trust Naila," Ahmir tells me. "She won't steal from us or try to hurt us. I know we'll be okay if we stay with her."

By the end of our stay, we have rallied Chan Hinge once more. I don't play a prominent role, only giving a small portion of one of the speeches, but I'm happy to support Ahmir. I'm not sure how I feel about him screaming at the crowd about killing our adversaries all the time, but I'm not incredibly involved, and it's only while we're in Chan Hinge. Once we leave, Ahmir says, we can return to our speeches about sound principles and moral values.

"Why don't you talk about that to these people?" I ask him.

"They're tired of hearing that stuff, Edelweiss. They like hearing about fighting because they're warriors. These will be our soldiers one day who fight the lands that disagree with us. There *has* to be a war, darling. You can't make change without fighting."

"I thought you wouldn't force people to join you."

"I won't," he replies, exasperated. "I'm not going to force them to do anything. I'm just going to stop them from attacking us. It's all defense. If they come quietly, there won't be any loss of life. But if they refuse and attack us, we must fight back." I shake my head. I don't want to argue with him, but I'm starting to think that the End Raiders are more vicious than they appear.

When we finally leave, we thank Naila for keeping us as houseguests. She doesn't say anything, just snorts and shakes her head. Terrance gives us each a hug and tells us to fight hard.

"Until the end," Ahmir replies with a smile. Clarence and Milee don't say anything. I really do hope that Terance doesn't die. He is such a sweet child and harmless as a kitten. In my mind, he deserves a long life filled with great joy. I have no idea if this will actually happen, but one can only hope.

As Ahmir and I leave Chan Hinge and wave goodbye to the End Raiders, I do just that. Hope.

Thirteen

The next time we see land, it is Bridger. Here, we stay at a hotel that everyone assures us is the best in the land. The building looks like it's been painted in gold. The magnificence of it is dazzling in the morning light but also blinding. I can't look at it straight without squinting and blinking, but I wish I could take it all in with my eyes wide open.

When we arrive inside, ten little girls dressed identically greet us, each carrying a small bouquet of edelweiss. They wear short white dresses with little pink flowers on them. Their hair is in curls, and on their heads are wreaths of edelweiss.

"Thank you, thank you," Ahmir says as the little girls pile their flowers into our arms.

"They're for you!" they squeal. We thank them again and again, smelling each bouquet. As we go up to our hotel room, the bellboy carries our things for us.

"That was quite the warm welcome," Ahmir whispers to me.

"Yes, but what will we do with all of these flowers?" I ask.

"I don't know, but I doubt they'd find out if we threw them away."

"Maybe they have a few vases," I suggest. Our hotel room is lovely, and everything is decorated in gold, but there are no vases to be seen, so we just throw the edelweiss away.

That morning, we go out into the town and find that Bridger, at least where we are, is a very wealthy place. All of the houses are more than one story high, and everyone is dressed in fine clothing. We go to a shop called "Cream and Saucer," where they sell everything related to tea. Everyone there bows to us and occasionally introduces themselves, using the phrase "your Highnesses" in every sentence.

For lunch, Ahmir and I eat at a restaurant specializing in pasta, something we have not had much of before. We eat yellow pasta, green pasta, and a strange purple pasta. It comes in many different shapes and sizes: round, thin, thick, and flat, all with names I can't pronounce.

We spend the evening in our hotel room, where the bellboy delivers dinner to our door. It's a corn and lamb casserole. After savoring the last delicious bite, Ahmir announces that he's "feeling good enough to do a two-step."

We dance for the next half hour, giggling and remembering the first night we danced together at Seth Sound's castle.

The next morning, we receive a letter from the queen of Bridger that we are to come to the town square at noon for a public meeting between the royalty. We arrive a little late and have to hurry there. We see the queen on a large, glamorous stage, her forehead wrinkled and her face red.

"I, Queen Marriam, at this moment extend my gracious kingdom, Bridger, to this young couple, Prince Ahmir and Princess Edelweiss," she proclaims, her arms lifted gracefully, a lofty smile on her face, and yet staring at us hatefully.

"Thank you," Ahmir says cooly.

"Well then, I will make an announcement," Queen Marriam informs us.

The crowd silences to catch the queen's words. "Please, fair people. Hear me when I say that we will *never* be part of the End Raiders, and we will *never* be part of the vicious action that the End Raiders are part of."

My cheeks turn red, and I turn with pleading eyes toward Ahmir, but his pocketed fists are balled with rage. After this strange introduction, we shake hands, though Ahmir grasps the queen's hand far too tightly. She scowls at me when turned away from the audience.

"Hello, people of Bridger," Ahmir begins. "My wife and I are honored to be here today. We are honored, not just because you invited us here, but because we have our differences, and you have still made an effort to welcome us into your home.

"My wife, Edelweiss, came from a place similar to where you are now. A place where your family, not just your immediate family, but your royal family too, disagree with a certain empire, the End Raiders. Just like Edelweiss, you don't question your family's ideas. But eventually, you must realize that it is okay to hold different beliefs from your parents, government, and people." At this, Marriam sucks in her breath as if she's about to interrupt.

"The End Raiders have been spotted throughout history for centuries. The End Raiders have added to the culture you have today. They were the ones who named the Realm. They were the ones who built the most important buildings in the kingdoms. The End Raiders were everywhere. They achieved something nobody else could: total rule. And they kept it for more than 200 years. This is a feat not easily forgotten, and it is not forgotten. Their legacy will continue to be told for-"

"Yes, wonderful," Queen Marriam finally interjects. "The End Raiders really are something, aren't they? Well, I think that that sums up this show. My name is Queen Marriam of Bridger, and I hosted this performance."

"Thank you all for coming," I call to the audience, and then we leave the stage. Ahmir starts walking away quickly, and I almost have to jog to keep up with him.

"She wouldn't even let us talk," he mutters, breathing heavily.

"Well, the crowd was really interested in what you had to say. Maybe later this week, you can give a nice speech."

"Likely," he replies sarcastically, and we go back inside the hotel. Compared to the temperatures in Le Beth, we have beautiful weather. The sun shines brightly, though there is a chill in the wind, so we mainly wear thin but long-sleeved material.

The next day, we return to the town square and stand on the stage. A small crowd gathers to watch, but within minutes, two men in official-looking uniforms tell us we aren't allowed to speak here without permission from the queen. Ahmir tries to argue, but eventually, he gives up.

"How are we supposed to rally these people if the queen won't even let us speak about the End Raiders?" he vents.

"What if we just talked off of the stage?" I suggest. Ahmir thinks about it for a second.

"No, I doubt the queen will allow us to do that either, and what if she kicks us out? We don't need any trouble, and she's already getting irritated with us." This is true. The queen *is* probably fed up with our End Raider speeches.

Nonetheless, we do end up making a stand on the street. Unfortunately, not many people realize that we're speaking, as we're not on a stage, and it only reaches maybe twenty-five people, none reporters or journalists, so the speech won't be broadcast. In our hotel room, Ahmir and I brainstorm ways to communicate our message to the people in Bridger.

"We could go house to house, knocking on people's doors and asking for their support," I say.

"Like a shoe salesman?" Ahmir replies. "We'll look too desperate."

"We could put up a sign inviting people to our hotel room, and anyone interested could come."

"No," Ahmir sighs. "I don't think they'll be allowed to go into the hotel without paying or something."

"How about just somewhere random, then?" I suggest.

"Do you really think the queen will like our putting signs up in her kingdom?" Ahmir asks. I sigh.

"Well, what ideas do you have?"

"I don't know," he hesitates. "Maybe we could get a local newspaper to print an article about the End Raiders." My eyebrows raise.

"Maybe," I agree. "You see, darling, I knew you could think of something."

"Yes, but I'm not sure it'll work."

"Only one way to find out," I mutter, and we drop the conversation to eat our dinner of stuffed fowl.

In the morning, we visit a newspaper printing site. A bell is attached to the door, and when we open it, it jingles merrily. The man operating the shop is young and black-haired with a slick black goatee. He wears a green fabric hat and a matching green apron.

"How do you do, sir," I greet the man politely. He bows slightly.

"Your Highnesses. What may I do for you today?" Ahmir steps into the small shop and shakes the man's hand.

"We were wondering if you could print an article about the End Raiders." The man swallows nervously.

"The queen would not like that, sir. You do not understand; she is very harsh about that sort of thing. She banned any positive news about the End Raiders. She says they are dangerous barbarians who have killed people for many generations."

"But sir, surely you cannot believe that, yourself," Ahmir says, astonished.

"It doesn't matter what I think, Highness. If I want to stay out of prison, I better do as the queen says." The man shakes his head to clear it of such terrifying thoughts.

"What is your name?" I ask him.

"Benjamin Drummond, but you can call me Benny."

"Well, Benny," I say calmly. "I think this queen, Marriam, is more barbaric than the End Raiders. She takes away your freedoms. She doesn't let you speak her mind."

"Yes, well, she was married into the throne." I don't see what importance this is, but I go along with it anyway.

"Yes, don't you see, Benny? You don't want *her* to rule over you for the rest of your life. If you only write this newspaper article, you might spark something that will lead to a new generation. A new freedom and liberty will come to you at last. Does that sound like something you want, Benny?"

There are actual tears in that man's eyes when he replies.

"Yes, it sounds wonderful." Ahmir gives me a little nod of approval.

"You sure sound like a politician," he whispers. I give him a little smile. Yes, I may sound like a politician, but I'm not. I'm just a wife who cares deeply about her husband's success. We spend the afternoon helping Benny write the article. When we're finished, it sounds simple and convincing.

I thank Benny for his help and leave the printing site. It's the first successful thing we have done concerning the End Raiders since arriving in Bridger. I reread it one last time, just to be sure it's perfect:

The End Raiders Make a Call for Freedom
by Benjamin Drummond

Those who live in Bridger know that our queen, Marriam, was married into the throne nine years ago and that her husband allows her to rule as she sees fit. However, his lenient monitoring of her power is contagious. The citizens of Bridger enable her to stomp over their rights and freedoms, but I, Benjamin Drummond, am proud to be the first to step out of the shadows. Voicing our rights is a part of being a community.

Let us not hide in fear of the queen. Marriam is not a god and should not be put above the rest of us. If she has value, she may add it, but we will not passively permit her to diminish our rights.

The End Raiders started this movement, and this call to action will bring to light just how little Marriam is protecting us and how much she is hindering us. We must see that the End Raiders support our freedoms and endeavors and would not strip us of that. They seek to rule for noble reasons, unlike the selfish heart of Bridger's queen, so let us put our faith in King Roe and his family of End Raiders. Until the end, we will stay true to ourselves.

The article is published two days later. Benny is eager to show Ahmir and me his work, and we all admire how it looks. We are still in his shop when three men, wearing the same official uniforms as the men who told us we couldn't be on stage, walk in.

"We are here for the arrest of Mr Benjamin Harper," one of the men says with a deep, commanding voice.

"Who are you?" Ahmir demands.

"The queen's personal guard," Benny whispers, the color drained from his face. "They're going to - arrest - me?"

"Are you Mr Harper?" the same man questions, pointing at Benny.

"Yes," he stammers, and the two other men grab him by the arms. I am paralyzed in shock, unable to do or say anything. Ahmir turns to Benny.

"I'm so sorry," he says. "We'll get you out, I promise." The officer turns to Ahmir.

"You and your wife are being exiled," the man informs us. Ahmir frowns.

"Exiled? We don't even live here. How can we be exiled on vacation?" he asks.

"I don't know, I don't make the orders; the queen does. I just carry them out," he replies, clearly baffled. "Men, bind the prisoner." Just like that, Benny is shackled and taken away to prison. His shop is closed down.

"This is horrible," I whisper to Ahmir, tears stinging my eyes. "How can the queen do this?"

"She can't," he mutters through clenched teeth. "I know she can't. I just need to find out how to stop her." I am thoroughly unconvinced, but we just stand where we are for the next few minutes, me sobbing while Ahmir holds me. I never meant to hurt our new friend. Now, it seems we've done everything to get him thrown in prison.

Returning to our hotel room, we find more of the queen's personal guard waiting for us. Ahmir is furious, but I feel too guilty and distraught for any other emotion.

"Excuse me, your Highnesses," one guard says, stepping forward. "By the order of Queen Marriam, you are hereby banned from Bridger for the next fifty years. You have five hours to leave. Thank you, and have a good rest of your day."

Ahmir opens his mouth to argue, but the guard silences him with a polite raise of his hand, and the guards leave.

In the next five hours, all we have time to do is round up our crew for leaving and pack up our things. I am crying on and off all day, and when I ask Ahmir what we will do about Benny, he just shakes his head and admits there is nothing we *can* do.

"But Ahmir," I plead.

"I know, I know, but horrible things happen every day."

"That's not what you said when you wanted to help the Browns," I accuse him.

"But there's nothing in my power to do for Benny."

"Yes, there is. You just aren't being helpful."

"Stop it, Edel. I know you're upset, but please don't take it out on me. I can't do anything." I close my eyes, calming down.

"I'm sorry," I say. "I can't believe how unfair the queen is being."

"I know. I guess some things just can't be prevented."

All the ideas and all the hopes that I told Benny are false. He's in prison now, with less freedom than ever. He is probably being oppressed by that terrible woman who calls herself the queen of Bridger. I can never forgive Queen Marriam for what she has done, nor can I forgive myself for convincing Benny to write that newspaper article. It hadn't needed to be done; now, it has done no good. *I* am the one at fault, to be sure.

We leave Bridger in the lowest of spirits. At night, Ahmir tells me that sacrifices must be made so more good can come out of it. He assures me that Benny's article has done wonders for the empire.

"Listen, if there was never any injustice, never any tragedies, there would be no need for change or a single strong government. Unfortunately, there are these things, and it's stories like Benny's that people need in order to realize that we *do* need the End Raiders." I nod, tears sliding down my cheeks and dropping on my pillow.

"Yeah," I agree. "I hope that other people can see it that way too." With that, we fall asleep together, but my dreams are troubled. My father shows prominently in them, and Benny appears multiple times. I hope that Ahmir knows what is best because I don't.

Fourteen

The last destination we arrive at before heading home is High Fire. When we get there, we are met by a marching band and a festival put together on our behalf. A jovial duke beckons us to come and celebrate our arrival. The plump, fifty-year-old man wears a very tall top hat and a constant dimpled smile.

"Hello, guests," laughs the duke, a little red in the face. "How are you today? Come, come, join the party. We're having a marvelous time!" Ahmir and I are greeted by cheers and applause. Everybody wears a proud smile, and everyone is having a good time. I stow away my still-damp mood and allow the corners of my mouth to rise.

Ahmir is beaming, too, and we clap along to the band's music like everybody else. I can tell immediately that our time in High Fire will be fun. We dance, laugh, and clap along for about an hour until the duke finally tells us to hop into the buggy, where we will ride to his palace.

"So, visitors," the duke begins. "Where should we start? Oh, yes. Where are my manners? My name is Charles, and you are?"

"Ahmir and Edelweiss, sir," Ahmir replies.

"Oh, such pretty names. My own children are Kirk, Sally, and Roger. They are such trouble, those three. Roger's the only one still at home. The dear boy is nineteen. But how old are you?"

"I am seventeen now, sir," I reply, for I did turn seventeen last month.

"I am eighteen," Ahmir answers. Duke Charles' eyebrows shoot way up.

"Then you're younger than my son and married! Dear me, I'm

sure you'll like my boy. He is just like you two. Quiet, but fun! And good-natured, my children, we mustn't forget that quality. My wife is good-natured, too, but dear me! She's a pretty one."

"I'd love to meet her," I say.

"I'm afraid you won't be able to. She's away visiting our daughter at the moment."

"So, how have your people responded to the End Raiders?" Ahmir jumps in.

"The- the End Raiders? Oh, let's see, what was that again?" Duke Charles asks himself, his face wrinkled in concentration. "Oh yes, they are those nasty little rats, aren't they? Well, fortunately, we have poison for them." For a second, I am horrified. Then I realize he is speaking about something entirely different than the End Raider empire.

"No, no," Ahmir corrects him. "It's not a rat species. *End Raiders.* The End Raiders are a large army who want to unite the seven kingdoms."

"Oh yes, of course," the duke gasps. "How could that have slipped my mind? Yes, now I see. Well, the people don't mind much because they're not half as common a sight here as in other places. We don't bother about them coming over here occasionally, just for a visit. Kind of like you, right, Ahmir?"

"Yes," Ahmir says. "But have they ever considered joining them?"

"Oh goodness no," the duke cries, shocked. "No, no, we like our king; he's my cousin. If the End Raiders took over the Realm, he wouldn't be king anymore, and we don't like that idea so much here. No, it's much better the way it is now."

Ahmir nods.

"I see. Well, that's that, I guess." I look into Ahmir's green eyes and see that he is discouraged.

When we get to the palace, the duke shows us to our rooms and leaves us to unpack our things. I turn to Ahmir.

"You want to give a speech tomorrow?" Ahmir stares out of the window a long time before responding.

"No," he sighs. "I don't know, Honey, let's just relax here for a while. These people don't care about disaster and devastation. All they care about is having a good time. You saw how they were all dancing around, playing their silly instruments. Let's just leave them alone."

I don't answer.

I know I *will* be the Raiders' Queen one day, and when that day arrives, I want it to go smoothly. I don't want to fight people all my life, and I don't wish for Ahmir to fight them, either. I want us both to relax, like when we met. Maybe it is how much toiling we've been doing during our honeymoon, maybe it's got something to do with Benny, but I'm beginning to get second thoughts about... what?

Perhaps that's part of the problem. I don't even know what I don't like, but there's something. Maybe it's the stress. Or the negativity of it all. We're always going to be battling people with opposing views. I wish everybody would agree that the End Raiders are good, and then Ahmir and I can have some peace. I know this won't happen without a struggle, but how I wish it would work like that.

We spend the ten days in High Fire participating in festivities and having fun, but then always come back to the palace with damp moods. Ahmir hasn't even mentioned the End Raiders to anyone since asking Duke Charles about it, and I'm sure that's not a good sign.

The next few days are either game nights, masquerade parties, a city tour, stargazing, picnics, or bird watching. Ahmir and I are entirely worn out by the end of our stay, but we thank everybody for the wonderful time.

We wave to everyone as our ship leaves, and at least two hundred people cram the shoreline, waving frantically back and shouting their goodbyes. You would think that Ahmir and I are good friends of theirs by the way they act. We don't know their names, though they are blowing kisses at us and telling us how much we will be missed.

The ship ride back is peaceful enough. Ahmir has relaxed from all the pressure, and I have given up mourning Benny's terrible fate. In fact, I try not to think of him at all anymore.

The closer we get to shore, the more eagerly Ahmir and I wait to see his family and our home. Seth Sound has seemed so far away, and though I haven't thought of his family much during the honeymoon, I am now itching to see them again. I want to play with Maddie Jane and Maddie Grace once more. I wish I could just reach out and hold baby Livingston again. I even miss Lotus, though our encounters have always been at desperate times. As for King Roe, I wish to see how pleased he is with our success in Cap.

When I wake up next to Ahmir and look out the window, I see a sliver of land peaking over the horizon.

"Ahmir, Ahmir, look outside," I exclaim, shaking him awake. Ahmir runs to the window, and a grin spreads across his handsome face.

"We're home!" he yells and hugs me tightly.

"Almost," I laugh. "We're almost home. What are you going to do first when we get there?"

"First? I'm going to hug my sisters. And then I'll go outside, to our garden, and I will pour over those flowers again."

"Yes, I know you love your flowers," I say, fondly remembering my first time there. Ahmir had pointed out the edelweiss to me. Though it had rained shortly after, the small beauty I had seen right before the storm had been enough to go without sunshine for a while.

We stand on the deck for hours, waiting for Seth Sound to get closer. Soon enough, the land is within swimming distance and we feel the salty breeze whip our hair.

When the ship docks, Ahmir takes my hand.

"Come, Edelweiss, let's go home," he says, and we walk off the ship together. The ride back in the carriage is agonizingly long, and as I lean on Ahmir and he puts his arm around me, a smile forms on my lips. I will be home again with my darling husband and his wonderful family. Maybe his father isn't *wonderful*, but didn't he kiss us goodbye when we first left for our honeymoon? Yes, and he wanted to meet me when I returned to the castle after Lizzie Kinling was arrested. He has shown his affection toward me in small ways.

When Ahmir and I leave the carriage, a large crowd awaits us. Ahmir and I grin at them. I see that Mr Greene is here, and when I do, I gasp and wave. He beams at me and waves back. I recognize a couple other people, and then I see King Roe. He smiles just a bit and motions for us to come his way. Maddie Jane and Maddie Grace are on either side of him- shrieking, giggling, and jumping up and down. I turn to Ahmir and see his expression is as gleeful as mine... until it turns to shock, just as a bullet pierces his heart.

He falls to the ground, blood gushing out of his chest. I scream and collapse to the ground by his side, trying to staunch the flow of the hot, thick liquid. My hands are sticky with it like biting into a red cherry and letting the juices flow down my arms. The only thought in my head repeats over and over again:

This can't happen. How can this happen?

People rush over and try to help, everyone screaming and carrying on. I look over my shoulder and see King Roe standing precisely where he was before, looking horrified and as white as the marble castle he lives in. Mr Greene has his hand over his mouth and is trying to get out of the way. People are throwing their bodies in front of the king and the princesses, including me, just in case the shooter goes for them, too.

But the shooter doesn't fire again. He has done his job. He doesn't even try to run; he is still standing there with his pistol held up. Pulling the trigger seems to have paralyzed him.

However blinded I am by the tears that sting my eyes, I can make out one thing: the shooter is my father. How much can you hate someone? If there is a limit, I have surpassed it.

Fifteen

A terrible loss feels like a never-healing, ever-oozing scab on your heart or a tainted stain on your soul, one that bleeds through your body and poisons you daily.

I am lying on a green velvet couch, dread pumping through me. The doctors took Ahmir away on a stretcher, and King Roe managed to detain me, dragging me inside. I am in the Green Room now and slowly beginning to realize there is blood all over me. Not my own blood, but my husband's.

How can this terrible thing happen? I, who suffered so much just to get here, am being stripped of my happiness at the hand of my torturer, the man who titles himself my father.

Ahmir isn't dead yet, I repeat to myself. Is he, though? I didn't check while I had the chance. I should have. I should have checked. The doctors came and took him so quickly.

They'll save him. They have to. He's the prince, and they're doctors. If he can be saved, the doctors will do it. They have tools and machines and everything they need. Some people survive gunshots. Ahmir will probably come out with nothing more than a scar. A scar on his chest, where his heart is. What if the bullet struck his heart? He has to be alive; they would have told me by now if he's not.

My mind twists in circles like this, over and over, panic surging through my body and then simmering down to a painful grasp. I feel as if I am bleeding internally, as if my father is driving a knife slowly through my shaking flesh. Maybe if I scream again, it will dim the pain.

I try it out, but my voice catches, and I'm so tired, I don't want to do this anymore. It has only been thirty minutes without an answer, and I am already submitting to the torture.

Somebody walks into the room. I frantically sit up to see who it is. It is a maid carrying a steamy bucket and a white rag on the rim. She puts a finger to her lips just as I'm about to speak. She dunks the rag into the bucket and places it on my forehead. I half expect it to soak up blood, but then I remember that the gash in my head is internal only. The cloth drips hot water, but it feels to me like fresh tears spilling into my hair. I cannot find it in me to cry, so the steady dribble of the warm cloth weeps for me.

I will the maid to speak of Ahmir, but she does not once utter a word. I must speak, I must vocalize my terror, but I can't talk. I cannot construct one sound to do me the good I need, and as I writhe, trying to recapture my escaped voice, the maid leaves in silence, snapping the door shut.

I am hopelessly alone for the next few hours, though the isolation may be for years, for decades, for as long as the End Raiders reign. Until the end, I may be segregated. Finally, the arrival of a tall and well-postured man disrupts my torment.

King Roe, who has regained his natural color and imperious stance, strides into the room, and looks down in what seems to me mocking disdain.

"Ahmir is dead. You may blame your father." The king may kill me now, and I do not care at this time.

"You pitiless man," I choke out, tears battling their way to spill out of me but hindered by some wicked force trapping them within. Roe raises his eyebrows, and I look into those terrifying green eyes that haunt me like Ahmir's spirit.

"You think you're the first in the Realm to suffer like this?" he asks. He doesn't know my loss. How could he?

I need somebody, anybody to share a fraction of my pain, so I throw together the most hurtful words I can muster.

"If anyone deserves a young death, it is you, except *nobody* will grieve for you," I cry. King Roe's hand flinches as if he is about to slap me, and I brace myself for a hit, but it never comes. Instead, he just shakes his head and sighs,

"One day, *Princess*, you'll know how shortsighted you are." One of his words gushes with sarcasm, and I realize what a mean thing he is. King Roe whips away from me and leaves.

I am beginning to think that maybe this entire world of humans is one cruel and terrible body. Perhaps the only goodness in the whole Realm comes from Ahmir's pure and true love, a love that has been thoroughly extinguished by my father. He is a beast I have always known to be dangerous, but I could never have imagined this agony he would have placed upon me.

I know I think these things deludedly, and I may be, as King Roe says, shortsighted, but right now, I do not see how anybody has enough audacity to call me out for a fault when my dearest husband is dead. Not just dead, but *murdered* by the man I ran away from, the man I have been struggling to escape from my entire life.

If I could not cry before, I can now, and I wail because my whole life, soul, and being have been stripped from my empty body. My heart pumps blood for bodily survival, not for any love, because I am already dead in that area. In fact, I feel as lifeless as Ahmir.

Glass shatters through me when the voice in my head calls out that name. I can't bear to hear his name, now with such a different meaning than before. I cannot rebirth the pain of hearing or thinking of my long gone life: lost in the past, masked by sorrow, coated in hatred, and wrapped with death.

I grieve all night, alone, as no more visitors come. The sun sinks slowly down beneath my window of view, and as the light dims, I know it is shying slowly from the horizon, not instantaneous like the death of my darling prince, but just as torturous, slowly drawing out the pain.

Why didn't the world slow down? If I had known, if only I had known, I would have soaked up the few precious moments with my prince. I would have savored the last days, and then it wouldn't be so horrible.

I didn't love him enough in his life. I never told him how much he meant to me. Maybe it is a good thing I am suffering now. It makes me more worthy of his undying love, something I never returned enough. That is why this is happening to me now. It is because I deserve it. I didn't do enough. It was never enough. How can he still love me even when I don't believe in his people? When I don't believe in his empire? When I don't believe in him?

These thoughts haunt me in the sleepless night brought about by terror and grief. The morning brings no comfort to me. The dim light is as tiring as the dark of night. There is no one in the world to care for me anymore. My only ally is dead, the only one who can do me any good. Let the terrible creatures drive me mad, but let me never forgive them for their horribleness. Why should I have to hold my temper in the face of horrors?

I rarely leave my bed for more than two weeks, never once speaking. I cannot imagine that I will ever be happy again, not complete happiness, as real as the kind I have experienced with my prince. How can I when the only source has perished?

The only word that sometimes sits on my tongue like a tiny snowflake is a name: *Everleigh.* In that name there is a story untold, and I should have asked it out of Prince Kurt, who recited the poem so mysteriously that day. I need it now; I crave to touch the spirit of the one who bled ink onto the paper and wove the sorry tale of Everleigh. If only I could lay a gentle hand on the passionate, suffering soul, I could ease some of my own terrible grief.

I cannot remember the poem so well; I only know how it touched me. If I do not find it, my heart will sizzle away, shrinking like cooked meat. It will char and burn until I am bitter and wasted, as I'm afraid I'm becoming.

To find Everleigh, however, I must get out of bed. I am lethargic and can't seem to push myself off the green couch that has held my weight for a fortnight. I fall out of it and crawl, shaking, to the door, where I fish around for the handle.

I am half blind from my stress and weak from sleepless nights. My body is as thin as it was before meeting the prince, for I am eating even less than I ever have in poverty.

I feel like a wounded animal limping its way to death, but I may be somewhat recovered, somewhat soothed, if I can find the verses that share my agitation. I am inching down the hallway like a toddler, determined to get to the library my husband once showed me, when I am waylaid by Roe.

"Get up, child, and be civilized." I keep my resolve never to speak again and ignore him. I keep my white knuckles to the ground, shuffling around him, but Roe grabs me by my wrists and makes me stand. I resist at first, but then I do as he says.

"That's a start," he says. I try to stumble away from him, but he pursues and detains me. "Speak, and I will let you go. Use your words."

I breathe heavily, fiercely staring down the corridor. I don't want to give in to him. I would much rather stay silent than feel the pain of speaking again, but the only way I will ever live is to get my hands on the poem of Everleigh. As I think this, I instantly know I must speak to Roe. Ahmir once told me he's a poet.

"I hate the End Raiders," I hear myself say, gravelly and hoarse. I hadn't meant to say it. I had intended to ask about the poem I desire, but there came a sudden urge to insult Roe, to make him angry. Roe searches my face; I don't know for what, but I steadily watch those torturous eyes that are so familiar and yet so much more horrible now.

"Why?" he asks plainly, as if genuinely curious.

"I don't know," I admit, tears rapidly filling in my eyes. "I just don't know anymore."

"Then why did you marry Ahmir?"

"I don't know," I repeat, as if it's the only phrase I can utter. "I loved him."

"How could you?" Roe says. "How could you love him with all your soul and all your being and yet hate everything he believes in? Everything he *is*? For he is the End Raiders, don't you see?"

"No." And I don't see. "He was never- he was purer- better- than the End Raiders. Oh, why? Why did it have to happen?" I get no response from Roe. He only gazes at me with those terrifyingly beautiful emerald eyes.

"I need a poem," I tell him.

"What poem do you wish to see?" Roe mutters.

"Everleigh," I answer, and as I hear that name called through the hallway, as I feel my lips form that perfect word, the heavy pain loosens just a little.

"Everleigh?" repeats Roe in a queer, almost fearful voice. "I don't know it."

"It's foreign," I tell him, as I have only heard it in frigid Le Beth.

"I don't have it or know it, but I have a poetry book which you might want to look at. I glory in a poet's work and savor its shocking language. Maybe you will feel the same way."

His eyes light up, and for the first time since I met him, Roe smiles. He shows me to the library, where he has a red-bound poetry book.

"Here," he says. "You can have it."

I am fascinated by the book and enchanted by its contents. Two hours go by, and as I read each line, my heart gets lighter and lighter until I have read almost half of the entire book, and tears spill into my eyes - pure, not poisoned tears. I feel almost like a soaring dove, even if I am really a blackened fire, and it is relieving.

Each poem teaches my heart strength and encourages me to continue even through my pain. One poem is about a phoenix rising from the ashes of its deceased self. I consider myself the dead phoenix. I wonder how to resurrect.

My great pains are eased, but not yet taken away. The terrible venom that has pounded through me ever since my prince's death now quiets. I slowly realize that my life is not over and that I am a seventeen-year-old girl with probably more than fifty years ahead of me.

I am going home. There is no question about it. The prince is dead, so technically, I am no longer royal and will return to my mother. My father is no doubt in prison, but that means I am going back to Vashti. There is no way to get out of this terrible trap, no conceivable way out. I will be with Vashti no matter how long it takes.

There may be detours, like fainting at work or marrying the prince, but I will always fall back to Vashti Marlow. My fate is not going to change, and I know it.

I decide to speak to Roe about it later, right now I have to worry about regaining my footing. The poetry book has inspired me to stay strong. Each poem, each stanza, each line, each word has pushed me to get a hold back on my life, to keep going, even though my beloved is gone and dead.

Though I am still battling my grief, and I am morally exhausted, I have hope that there is still a life for me. I must dutifully take it, even if I wish to be resting eternally with my husband. I believe the dead are more privileged than the living.

Sixteen

I begin to pack my things the following morning, taking many items belonging to the castle because everything I own is Ahmir's or his father's. I find an envelope behind my desk as if someone had accidentally knocked it over. Reaching down to get it, I realize it is a letter I haven't yet read:

To Edelweiss Chapel
From Mother

I don't want to open it, but curiosity gets the better of me. Tearing it open, a paper cut slices across my index finger.

"Ow!" I yell and suck on the cut. I straighten the paper and read it to myself.

Dear Edelweiss,
I know you are angry with your father and me, so you ran away. We looked for you everywhere but only found a small scrap of your dress. I taped it to my journal, reminding me of you constantly. It has been weeks since you left, and yesterday, I received the news that you are marrying the prince. I don't know how that happened or why you have decided to do it, but let me warn you: Do not marry this man if it is out of vengeance for your father. Your father will be hurt, but so will many other people, including yourself and your husband. I'm glad you are growing up to make decisions independently, but such a sudden and risky one may lead you into trouble. Edelweiss, I do not tell you this to

control or beg you to come home but simply to warn you. You have only just met the prince. He has his own agenda that you may not be aware of. Don't let him use you. Be careful, my daughter. No matter what you do, I will always love you. So will your father, even if he shows it differently.

Affectionately,

Mother

I barely have time to digest this before King Roe enters the library in his usual sullen manner.

"I need to talk to you," he tells me. I look him in the eyes, the painful eyes of my husband, and wait for him to speak.

"Ahmir's death has upset many people," he begins. "If something is not done, they will lose favor in our cause. Therefore, you must not disappear; you must show your support, symbolizing the strength and persistence of the End Raiders." Dread fills my insides. My eyes ache to see the familiar landscape of my childhood instead of this marble-white castle, stripped of its original excitement and hope.

"Why?" I demand. It is rude to say this to a king, but I have lost all interest in manners.

"Because they like you and trust you. They want you to assure them that everything is alright." I clench my teeth.

"Everything is not alright."

"I don't care. Do as I say, and you will be glad you did." He turns around and stalks out of the library. I stare at the cover of the poetry book, seething. Every bone in my body aches to leave the castle, but now I cannot. Even Vashti sounds bearable compared to this new fate.

I leave the library and go to the Dining Room to eat lunch, realizing this is the first time I have done so since I was single. I am greeted by Maddie Jane and Maddie Grace, who are extremely quiet, and a maid brings in Livingston. I offer to feed the baby for her.

"Thank you," she says with a grateful smile. "And I'm sorry... about your husband." My mouth goes dry, and I find it impossible to swallow.

"Yes," I agree, and the maid leaves. I probably should say more, but I can't think straight right now. A server brings in baby food and three cold turkey sandwiches. I feed Livingston first and then eat my own food.

"Edelweiss!" Maddie Grace says tentatively.

"Yes, Maddie?"

"How come you haven't left your room until now?" I don't know what to tell the little girl, who wouldn't understand the depth of genuine pain.

"You know how sometimes you get sick and feel like staying in bed all day?"

"Yes," the twins say.

"It's like that, except it's not a physical illness. It's in my heart." They look at me with their big blue eyes but don't say anything more.

I can't get down more than a few bites, so I abandon the rest of the plate and bring Livingston into the Yellow Room to nap.

I sit on the yellow couch for an hour, staring at the content baby, tranquil in his sleep. The twins work hard at drawing something on a piece of paper. After a while, they grin as they show it to me. It's a sketch of me, wistfully watching their baby brother.

"It's beautiful," I tell them. "Why did you draw it?"

"We thought it would cheer you up," Maddie Jane says. "You've been so sad recently. Isn't there something we can do?" I smile and hug them both.

"Keep being cheerful, I suppose. Maybe one day it will rub off on me." They beam as King Roe intrudes again and asks for my attention.

"You will give a speech tomorrow morning," he informs me. I scowl at his feet.

"I have nothing to say," I tell him without looking up.

"You don't have to. Your script has been written for you."

"Where should I give it?" I snap.

"At a graveyard. Many important eyes will be watching, so do good." I shift my jaw left and right, still staring at Roe's shiny black shoes.

"I'm not your puppet, and I won't be your slave," I reply. The king rolls his eyes.

"It's not about you. It's about the End Raiders."

"I don't care about your stupid End Raiders." I feel the muscles in my stomach contracting and my arms shaking.

"It doesn't matter. You *will* deliver the speech."

I shake my head.

"You can't make me," I insist, even though he can.

"Try me, child," he challenges. "You can do as I say, or you can end up with your father." The mention of that hateful title forces me to gasp. My eyes well up with tears, and my shoulders shake, but my father-in-law just walks away, leaving me alone again. I think about the location of my speech, and fear clenches me.

The next morning, a maid lays out a black dress on my bed. It is a glossy ball gown with lace sleeves that fall to the floor. I wear a veil with the same edelweiss pattern as my wedding veil, except it is black. The maids curl my hair as I stare at the long dress below me. Though it feels silky against my skin, my body shrinks away from it. I shutter at the way its blackness consumes me, trapping me in my mind's dark thoughts.

I get into a carriage with King Roe, who's in a black tuxedo. Maddie Grace and Maddie Jane sit on either side of me, leaning against my arms. Livingston is left at home. We ride in silence, though Roe hands me my script, and I read over it once. With each word, I increasingly dread delivering it to the public.

When we finally arrive, I step out to greet hundreds of figures wearing black. They all have solemn and yet eager expressions smeared across their faces. King Roe throws an arm around me and guides me to the graveyard, where the ceremony is being held. I hate the pressure around my torso as if he is binding me, but I don't resist him.

I spot an area where a hole has been dug. At the front of it, a grave-stone stands. It reads:

Prince Ahmir
of Seth Sound and the End Raiders
Forever remembered by his father, sisters,
grandmother and wife,
along with his empire and his kingdom.
May the Raiders reign on in his absence
Until The End

I bite my lip as I read it and then turn my eyes away from the epitaph. A second later, I wish I hadn't because my sight rests on an open casket, with my husband's lifeless form lying inside.

I only glimpse it briefly, but its effects are immediate and eternal. Though my eyes scream to see the dirt, the image from a second ago is burned into my vision. I can still see the hollow cheeks marble white, the corpse still and unmoving, the gorgeous, lion-like hair flat and blanched, everything about him limp and dead.

My memory flashes back to the day he was shot. I remember turning to see that he was smiling, then the bullet piercing his chest and his expression shocked. I can see him tumbling over, thumping to the ground. I, dropping to my knees, watched the blood flow out of him and saw my father with his gun, a satisfied expression carved onto his face.

King Roe grasps my arm and leads me to a podium, where I am to give my speech. I swallow, sickened by what I have just seen, and turn my attention to the sky. The sun is hidden slightly by a cloud, though most of the ether stretches on for miles of blue.

I lower my head to focus on the script in front of me. The crowd is silent and still, all eyes cast on me: the princess at the podium.

"Greetings," I say finally, though my tone is uninviting, and my volume is small. I take a breath and speak a little louder.

"I wish that we did not have to be here today on account of my husband's death. Such is life. Hoping. Wishing. Complaining. But no matter how much time we spend doing those things, we are here, so we may as well say goodbye to Prince Ahmir, good and faithful to his kingdom, to his empire, to his father, and to me." I pause because my mouth is so dry.

"The reason we are here today is because of my father, hateful and unfeeling. He, the man who opposed the End Raiders for so long, murdered his own son-in-law in the face of anger. These are our enemies. People like my father toss away all the love in the world because of their hatred. Many say the End Raiders are like my father, but we are not. We strive for peace and non-violence." I stop, not only because I have no saliva left but also because I am trying to think if what I am saying is true.

Are the End Raiders against violence? I know that Ahmir was. But I also know they start wars, murder people who disagree with them, and burn books to spread terror. I begin to shake, something I have been doing often since my husband's death.

"I hate people," I say in the same voice I used when I told Roe I hated the End Raiders, and I know that every member of the wretched audience is asking each other and themselves if they heard me right. I glance at King Roe, who looks furious. "I do," I mutter, but not quietly enough for people to miss. Anger and a burning need to justify myself rise up.

"I hate them because they're liars and hypocrites, and they shun other people for doing bad things, but then they do them too. They're greedy and motivated by self-interest. They're haters, and snobs, and cheats, and they're tempered, and I'm sick of the likes of them." King Roe strides up to the podium, his face red and eyebrows knitted . I don't stop, though, and he's far enough away to get in a few more sentences.

"One of the beasts is trying to stop me now. How dare I speak the truth? How dare I stop uttering false flattery to a stupid, selfish cause, where the rich are the winners, and the poor are the losers?" King Roe is almost at the podium. I speak faster and louder, trying to get in everything I must say.

"Nobody cares about you. I don't care about you. No government does, either. Why should we? You're a scoundrel as much as the rest-" I am cut off, and an iron-tight arm yanks me from the podium, but I don't fight it. I have said my part, and there is nothing that Roe, or anyone else, can say to change the truth.

After I finish speaking, a commotion breaks out over the crowd. Everyone watches in amazement as their king stuffs me into the carriage and barks at me to stay there. He, flushed and dangerous, marches up to the podium. I do not dare to break loose from the carriage, and I simply look out the window and listen as King Roe apologies and makes a lame excuse for my behavior.

"When we suffer losses, we often act out in rage. It is all part of mourning, but we must learn to accept that blaming people is unhealthy. I am sorry that I did not realize how unprepared the princess was, fresh from the shock of her husband's death. Widows should be supported in their healing and forgiven when they have a momentary lapse of sanity. Princess Edelweiss is of yet unstable and extremely sensitive. We must respect that. Thank you for your time."

The ceremony continues, but I wonder if anybody pays much attention. I don't regret my words yet, but a pang of guilt for my betrayal troubles me. As soon as Ahmir dies, I turn my back on him and go against his people.

An hour or so later, King Roe waves to the audience and gets into the carriage. As soon as he is out of view from the people, he grabs my arm in a bone-crushing hold.

"You will pay," he threatens without releasing me. "And you will be sorry." I stare into his enchanting eyes so that I will not be disgusted by his other harsh features.

"No," I reply. Now that the heat of anger has dissipated, I am cold, quiet, and slightly hoarse. "You will pay. You're already paying right now. Everyone hates you, you know." He thrusts my arms away from him.

"Nobody believes your weak story," he scoffs, but I know he's lying. He is afraid I have done severe damage to his empire.

I go to bed that night feeling slightly relieved and satisfied, but there is still another part of me that is tired, weak, and injured. The fight has left me, and only an ache remains. Pain is often masked by anger, but anger is fleeting. Pain lasts much longer.

The following two days, I become more active, taking walks through the garden and playing with the princesses. They are now my greatest joys, and I have to admire their resiliency to their brother's death.

"Why can't everybody just be nice?" sighs Maddie Jane. I smile wistfully.

"Are you always nice?" I ask.

"No," she admits.

"Then you can't blame anyone else," I say. Roe comes into the room.

"Yes?" I ask in a hostile voice as Maddie Grace runs to her father. He strokes her head but addresses me.

"I have decided what to do about you."

"What?" I spit at him, tearing my attention away from the book and looking into his face.

"You will marry me," he answers simply. My heart skips a beat.

"You can't do that," I sputter, unconvinced. "I won't marry you. Never." King Roe smirks.

"What choice do you have? Where are you going to go?"

"Home," I reply.

"What home? Your father will be in prison for the rest of his life. He's there now. Your mother is dead. You have no other family." My next sentence comes out hollow.

"My mother is dead?"

Roe nods.

"She died a week before your father murdered Ahmir. She was sick." For some reason, this news doesn't hit me like a new tragedy but like the old scar reopening, and it aches all over again. I am getting hurt so often these days that it hardly shows on my face anymore.

"It doesn't matter," I tell him. "None of it matters."

"Then you will marry me," he replies.

"Yes," I give in.

"You will be the queen," he persists.

"Yes. But be sure my father is aware of it." It is a poisoned bit of revenge to torture my father with, but I can't help it. Roe smiles.

"Yes, I will tell him personally."

"Good then. Leave me now."

"Edelweiss, let me first talk to you." He sits beside me on the couch and stares into my hazel eyes. "I don't mean to make you miserable."

"Is that so? You sure act like it."

"I think you make yourself more pathetic than you could be. You know I lost a spouse, too."

"But this is different. I didn't murder Ahmir." Roe looks away from me and doesn't know what to say. I continue. "Ahmir told me you bullied her into doing what you wanted. You don't even know what love is."

The king shrugs and leaves. I don't feel bad for him because I am trapped, not him. My only option is to marry the king. I have to live with that.

Seventeen

I am wearing the same white wedding dress, I have on the same edelweiss-patterned veil, the maids apply the same unfamiliar makeup and do the same curled and plaited hairstyle, we're going to the same church, and yet, my second wedding is nothing like my first. I'm not nervous or excited; I'm not happy or hopeful. I am sitting in the Yellow Room with my two bridesmaids beside me, and I am seething.

"Edelweiss?" Maddie Grace asks. I turn my head. "Does this mean you're our mother now?" Both of the girls stare at me.

"Stepmother," I say. "How old are you?"

"We'll be eleven next month," Maddie Jane answers.

"Then I'm not even seven years older than you," I reply. "I'm more of a sister than a mother, really."

"I like that," Maddie Jane tells me. "Sister Edelweiss." We sit for another fifteen minutes before a maid comes in.

"Are you ready, your majesty?" the maid asks. I hesitate.

"Yes."

We ride to the church in a carriage, King Roe across from me.

"Why do you always look so despondent?" he criticizes. "Nothing bad has happened to you in months." I look out the window to see a crowd waving at us, all trying to get a glimpse. Roe mutters something I can't understand just as the carriage stops. He opens the door for his daughters and me before climbing out. The twins beam as he waves his hand to the assemblage.

I cast my eyes to the ground, scowling against the bright sun. We enter the church together, hand-in-hand. Everyone's eyes follow us as we march up the aisle. The priest addresses us, and the orchestra stops playing.

"Do you, Roe, king of Seth Sound and the End Raiders, take this woman to be your lawfully wedded wife, to live together in matrimony, to love her, comfort her, honor and keep her, in sickness and in health, in sorrow and in joy, to have and to hold, from this day forward, as long as you both shall live?"

"I do."

"Do you, Edelweiss, princess of Seth Sound and the End Raiders, take this man to be your lawfully wedded husband, to live together in matrimony, to love him, comfort him, honor and keep him, in sickness and in health, in sorrow and in joy, to have and to hold, from this day forward, as long as you both shall live?"

The priest is silent. The crowd is silent. I am silent.

"Say it," whispers Roe, his lips unmoving. I think about my late mother, who always wanted me to do well in life; Vashti, whom I have narrowly escaped on several occasions; Ahmir, who would have hated his father for this; and my own father, paying his price in prison.

"I do." I have to shove the words out of my mouth, but at least I say them. The onlookers clap. King Roe and I slip the rings onto our fingers. We take the priest's place at the podium and give a little speech that has been scripted for us. I am careful to say each word as it is in the script. I don't, however, try to put any feeling into the performance, muttering most of the words.

We eat dinner at the reception and then meet with important people. I stand silently as Roe talks to an End Raider general when the steady clink of a spoon against glass meets my ears. Queen Lotus stands at the podium, lifting a glass of champagne.

"Attention, everyone," she declares. "A long time ago, my son married the love of his life. When she died, she left my boy with only a shadow of grief. Today, that shadow is lifted as his daughter-in-law, Edelweiss, brings him the happiness he has sought." I raise my eyebrows as everyone throws back their glass.

"I'm surprised your mother can lie that well," I tell Roe between sips of champagne.

"It's easier when you have a script," he responds, chuckling.

"It's not funny." I wrinkle my face into a scowl. Roe looks at me and laughs harder.

"You take everything so seriously. I thought it was a well-written message."

"Let me guess. You wrote it," I accuse.

"No, I didn't."

"Who did, then?" I await an answer, but Roe only shakes his head, still chortling. "Come on, tell me." When he is still silent, I slap his arm.

"Alright, alright," he consents. "I offered the criminals at the OAR (Offense Against the Royals) prison an opportunity to get out a month earlier. Your father was there. He told me he'd rather die. Lizzie Kinling wrote it, the girl my son almost married. She says you know her." I gasp, having almost forgotten Lizzie.

"She wrote that?" I ask in amazement.

"Yup. I thought she did a great job."

"Lizzie was both a friend and an enemy to me," I tell him wistfully.

"Kind of like me?" he inquires. I frown.

"No. Not at all like you." I stride away from him and approach the twins, who are rubbing their eyes and yawning.

"It's been a long day, huh?" I ask with a smile.

"I'm so glad you're marrying Father," Maddie Jane says. "Now we have two parents again."

"I'm happy for you," I say. "I hope I don't disappoint."

"You won't," Maddie Grace assures me. "You're too wonderful."

Soon, the wedding ends, and we ride back to the castle. I'm going to the Green Room when King Roe comes from behind me.

"Edelweiss," he calls out.

"What is it?"

"Your coronation is in two weeks."

"Oh good," I reply sarcastically.

"Most girls would do anything to be in your place."

"Really? Would most girls do anything for their fathers to shoot their true love right in front of their eyes? Would most girls do anything to marry a beast?"

"You mustn't say such things, child, or you will be punished."

"Then punish me and enjoy the pleasure. Maybe it'll kill me. I'd be glad of it."

"I don't want to hurt you," Roe retorts. I roll my eyes and give a short, sharp laugh that is not mine.

"Of course you do. You hate me."

"You hate yourself."

I am silent, tears spilling into my eyes. Roe notices and sighs. I expect him to apologize, but he doesn't. He doesn't even seem sorry for what he has said.

"Can I go to bed now?" I ask.

"What's stopping you?" he answers, turning away.

I enter the Green Room and slam the door hard enough to echo through the hallway.

The next day, I eat breakfast alone. I wonder where the princesses are, and I'm about to search for them when King Roe enters the Dining Room.

"Where are your daughters?" I ask.

"They're halfway to Odin Boarding School by now," he replies cooly.

"What?"

"I sent them to boarding school at 4:00 this morning."

"Without saying goodbye?"

"I said goodbye."

"But not to me?"

"Why would I need to say goodbye to you? You're not going anywhere."

"You know what I mean," I snap impatiently. "Why didn't the princesses say goodbye to me?"

"You were asleep."

"I don't care!"

"You weren't awake to tell them that."

My eyes fill with tears.

"You know I love them," I accuse. "You sent them away to hurt me. Say that you did!"

"Even if I did, it doesn't make me worse than you. *You* went on a rant against humanity to hurt me."

"You deserved it."

"But you didn't?"

"I hate you. Why do you insist on taking every small pleasure from me?"

"The girls should hardly be a *small* pleasure."

"You know what I mean," I say for the second time, tired of him pretending he doesn't understand what I'm talking about.

"And you know what *I* mean."

"Yes, you mean to punish me for speaking the truth over my husband's dead body."

"That's quite the accusation."

"You're a meanspirited, revengeful man."

"Much unlike you, hypocrite. You're always seeking revenge on your father."

"He murdered my husband!"

"He was *my* son, but I'm not pouting over it."

"That only proves you're hard-hearted."

"No, it proves I'm resilient. I'm the End Raider's king, child. Ahmir's death was not the end."

"It was the end of my joy."

King Roe pauses for a moment.

"Go away. It's draining to see you like this," he dismisses me. I stalk away and cry in the Green Room.

Everything becomes lonelier after our conversation, and I feel my recovery from Ahmir's death begin to slip away. My heart aches worse, and I find minimal enjoyment in anything.

The day of my coronation feels like a third wedding, this one just like the second. The only difference is that it isn't matrimony to Roe but to Seth Sound and the End Raiders.

An old, haughty-looking man places a silver crown on my head, glittering with tiny diamonds, rubies, and sapphires. Then I give a coronation speech.

"Dear people of Seth Sound, loyal followers of the End Raiders, today I pledge to serve you for as long as I reign, and you swear to aid and obey me. I will treat my kingdom and my empire with respect and grace. I will protect, support, and defend it at all times. I will stand alongside my husband, the king, and we will help you through the good times and the bad.

"I promise to be fair, loyal, peaceful, and daring. I will not fight for the sake of war but for the sake of my people, if necessary. My promise to you is to be kept until the end." It is a short acceptance speech, probably so I don't blow up halfway through like I did at the funeral.

King Roe nods his satisfaction. I know that no matter how many speeches I give, none will ever heal the damage I have already caused, but it makes my husband feel better.

"How was I?" I ask him mockingly.

"It was definitely an improvement from the graveside tirade," he tells me, smiling almost warmly. "You are slowly getting better, Edelweiss. Soon, you will leave your mourning period and return to life."

"That's what you hope, at least.".

"Yes, and I usually hope for plausible things."

The next day feels strange, even stranger than when I became a princess. Being the queen has an unfamiliar ring, like I am powerful, even though I have less control than ever. I am reading more of the poetry book in the library when Roe enters the room.

"Explain this," he says, shoving a newspaper under my nose.

Protests Against King Roe and the End Raiders

Protesters flood the streets, carrying signs bearing titles such as "Our Monarchy is Mental," "End Raiders are Cruel," and "Riot Against Roe." Ever since Prince Ahmir's funeral, many rumors have risen about the royal family. The leading theory is that Queen Edelweiss is mentally unwell. The king is suspected of exploiting this by extracting pity and attention from the Realm to keep the End Raiders in the public eye.

Seth Sound, previously devoted to King Roe, is raging up against him. Chan Hinge, the Raiders' headquarters, considers cutting off their alliance with the empire. Cap, the newest kingdom under the End Raiders' hold, does not favor their king's decision to surrender. Known as the Land of Philosophy, Cap's citizens are giving the new End Raider leaders pushback.

The Realm is coming to realize, through Queen Edelweiss's conflicted actions and the death of Prince Ahmir, that the End Raiders may not be living up to their promises. Some even go as far as to question the survival of the End Raider monarchy. We hope to find out more soon.

"I don't know," I say simply.

"You don't know what?"

"I don't know why they believe that." King Roe shakes his head.

"You are getting to be a whole lot of trouble, young lady."

"I don't know why you married me, either. If you had just let me go, nobody would care anymore. That's your mistake, not mine."

"If you disappeared, everyone would get their hopes dampened; they would be outraged at our family's weakness. Ahmir was supposed to marry you to bring novelty to the End Raiders, but now you've just caused turmoil and hurt feelings."

"I know," I say, staring at my hands. I don't precisely lament this new turn of events, but I wish things could be peaceful; I hate having to worry about politics and other peoples' opinions which I have no control over. When I don't say anything more, King Roe snatches up the newspaper and leaves me.

It's hard to believe that somewhere in the Realm, people are fighting with all sorts of delusions in mind. This is all because of what they don't know and what they think they know. The Realm would be a much clearer place if everybody kept in mind this objective thought trail: what they know and what they don't.

Eighteen

I lay on the couch, twirling my finger around my hair. Nobody has spoken to me all day, I haven't left bed for hours, and I have had no responsibilities since my coronation. Some people may think this is paradise. I am not one of them.

I have to consider getting out of bed and going to dinner for several minutes before starting the process. I shuffle my feet in the hallway and am surprised to see King Roe waiting at my usual table.

"Come on," he hurries me. I make an extra effort to walk as slowly as possible. When I finally arrive, he scowls.

"You have a terrible attitude for a queen."

"I didn't want to be a queen."

He shakes his head.

"I will eat dinner with you from now on."

"What are you punishing me for this time?" I groan.

My husband doesn't answer, possibly because he is distracted by the arriving food, but probably because he is too annoyed with me. We are served bread, jam, and turkey jerky.

"What," Roe demands, holding up a jerky strip. "Is this?"

"Turkey," the waiter replies quietly. "Your majesty, we don't have fresh meat right now."

"Excuse me? Is this a castle or a peasant's village?"

"Your majesty, please," the waiter begs. "There's nothing we can do. We're in a shortage."

"What?" King Roe bellows, slapping the jerky back on his plate. "We've never had shortages before."

"Yes, sir, I understand, but our supplier is refusing to give us meat right now."

"Why?"

"I don't know, your majesty. I'm just the waiter."

"Get the chef in here. Now." The waiter whisks himself away, and King Roe faces me.

"If this is a protest, and it's your fault..." he threatens. I drop my gaze to the floor just as the chef comes in.

"What is this I'm hearing?" growls King Roe.

"Yes, sir, I'm sorry, but like Turner said, the supplier is stubborn, and we can't get the meat from him."

"That's outrageous."

"I'm sorry."

"'Sorry' doesn't get me my dinner."

"Your majesty, the jerky is delicious, especially with the bread and jam. Have some!"

"Get me my *real meat* in two days, or you will be out of a job." The chef bites his lip.

"Of course, your majesty."

The chef retreats to the kitchen. King Roe closes his eyes.

"Do you have any idea what you have done, my child?"

"I have spoken the truth."

"You have wrecked my kingdom."

"You have wrecked my heart." The bright green eyes flash open, and my heart skips a beat at how brightly they blaze.

"*I have?* I have wrecked your heart? I have done nothing to you. I have let you into my home. I have allowed you to marry my eldest son, though you were nothing more than a broke villager. I have not banished you to the streets like I should have, but I have made you my queen instead. What more do you want from me?" he shouts.

I leave the room without touching my plate.

Over the next week, the quality of our meals declines. Soon, King

Roe and I are eating only bread and preserved foods. Our chef is fired, but it doesn't matter. He might as well have kept his job. Our dinners are no better.

One day, while I am reading my poetry book in the Yellow Room, King Roe barges in.

"Come and tell me what you see." Curiosity drags me from the couch and forces me to walk with King Roe. We go up a winding case of stairs, ones I've never been on, up to a balcony.

"Look," he commands. I peer over the balcony's edge and see that it overlooks the surrounding city. I can discern rural farmland in the distance, but closer to the castle is a thick urban area. I look almost directly down and have to squint to notice the movement beneath me. What I discover takes my breath away.

There is a mob of people half a mile out from the castle. End Raider soldiers fight them off, and blood is all over. I can hear gunshots and see people collapsing.

"Oh no," I breathe.

"Look what you have started," King Roe says. "I construct a successful army, and you destroy it."

"Oh no," I repeat, hardly hearing Roe at all. "The End Raiders are killing them."

"Those rioters, my dear, are trying to kill *you*."

"No, they're not. They're only fighting because they think they know, but they don't. They're coming for you, not me. You're the manipulative one. I'm the one they pity."

"No, Edelweiss. They fed on your lies, and you fueled them, but they are stronger than you are. They will prey on you and kill you like the rest of us."

"You're wrong," I whisper.

"We'll see."

I am too preoccupied thinking about the protesters to read my poetry book. Is it true they hate me as much as Roe? Before being on the balcony, I had considered myself their ally. But I may be just another

End Raider to them- telling a new tale, spinning a new story. After all, I *am* the Raiders' Queen.

At dinner the following day, King Roe shows me another newspaper.

Raiders vs Rioters: The End Is Coming

"Until the End." This is the End Raiders' motto. It seems, however, that the Raiders' time is coming to a close. Seth Sound is divided, with a majority ready for mutiny. King Roe has refused to leave his castle and has not spoken since his wife's coronation. Queen Edelweiss is stubbornly hating everyone, with no help to either side. It appears she is more than a sorrowful widow- many believe she is a madwoman being manipulated by her husband to appear victimized.

Experts suggest this is not a new strategy of King Roe's, as this behavior mimics the dynamic between King Roe and his late wife. Individualists (those against the Raiders) around the Realm hold their breath in anticipation of Edelweiss's untimely death. Some even go so far as to theorize that King Roe was behind Prince Ahmir's murder.

Currently, the castle is restricted from food, groceries, and necessary items until the king and queen agree to leave their hiding hole and tell the public the truth.

"I'm sure they love you, mad woman," King Roe smirks.

"I never needed their pity."

"Do you not care at all about your own life?"

"What does my life have to do with this? If they commit mutiny, I'll just go home and marry Vashti."

King Roe bursts into an outrageous cackle.

"What did you say?"

"I said I'll go home."

"No, you will die."

"What, are you going to kill me? They say you will, right here." I point to the section about my "untimely death."

"Oh no, my queen! I'm not a murderer. No, I will do my best to keep your life going for as long as possible, but eventually, they will execute us both."

"What? No, they won't. Stop talking nonsense."

"Oh yes, they will. If they overpower us, we will be slaughtered, along with Maddie Jane and Maddie Grace and Livingston and Lotus. It will be just like my father Leroy, like your husband Ahmir, except it will be all of us." A small silence follows his words.

"What have I done?" I whisper, believing Roe. The king shakes his head.

"What have you done indeed?" He stands and stalks out of the Dining Room, while my horror further consumes me. For the first time, I realize the full extent of my words and their impact. I have not only hurt my husband but myself and his entire family. I have damaged the whole kingdom. The whole Realm. I have turned order into chaos, and I *will* pay for it.

The next morning, I am awoken by a sharp knocking at my door. I look out the window, but only a sliver of green light squeezes through the curtains. I moan as I get out of bed and trudge to the door. King Roe is in an official-looking uniform, decked out in badges and awards. He cradles his son, Livingston, whose sleeping head rests against his shoulder.

"What is this?" I ask in confusion. "It's so early." The king hands me a large bag.

"Put everything on, and we'll go up the stairs to the balcony I showed you. We're going to see the people."

"What if they shoot us?" I ask.

"Don't worry, Edelweiss. We will have maximum protection. Now, hurry up. We don't want to keep people waiting." He shuts the door, and I put the bag on the bed. As I unbutton it, silky fabric explodes from the pack. I pull it, and a very long dress emerges. I take off my pajamas and replace them with the strapless frock.

I rummage through the other contents, and my fingers hit something bulky and metal. Straining to lift it up, I find a metal corset. My loud groan echoes through the Green Room. I slip off the dress, manage to strap myself in the iron corset, and put the dress back on.

"Are you done yet?" Roe shouts from the door.

"What's with the corset?" I yell.

"It's bulletproof," he answers. *Of course*, I think, and suddenly I wish I could wear a full set of knights' armor instead of the skimpy torso protection. I wrestle the dress's matching gloves on and squeeze my feet into a pinched pair of heels. It's the first time I'm wearing heels since that hot August day- almost two years ago.

"Okay," I shout while securing a gold and emerald tiara to my head. "I'm ready."

"Finally," Roe grumbles as I limp toward him. "What's the matter?"

"These heels. They're so tight," I say. They *are* narrow, but the reason for my hobbling is my lack of heel adequacy.

"And your dress is too long," he notices. I look down to see the ends draped along the floor.

"Oh, I'm stepping on it," I say and attempt to adjust. The lace snags my shoes, and I begin to stumble. I try to lift my dress, but I just trip over myself. Roe barely flinches as he catches me around the shoulders, still holding Livingston with an arm.

"Thank you," I say, scowling and carefully untwisting the gown. Roe pulls something out of his pocket and wordlessly hands me an old photograph. A man and woman stand together on a balcony with a little boy in the man's arms. I recognize the man as Roe. The strawberry blonde-haired lady beside him has on the same outfit as I do. She wears a dimpled smile and confidently postures her tall, thin frame. I don't recognize her, but she seems familiar.

"It's my wife and I with Ahmir. I'm hoping the reenactment will be seen as an acknowledgment to her. It might calm them down some."

"I hope so," I reply, wobbling as I walk up the steps. "But the balcony is too tall and far to speak from."

"The only thing you have to do is smile, wave, and look sane," he assures me.

"That's been rather challenging recently," I say, stepping onto the terrace. Shouts greet my ears, but I'm unsure whether they are out of anger or approval. My husband comes up from behind, smiling.

"Pretend you like me," he whispers, putting his arm around my waist. I shutter at the vulnerable feeling of my uncovered shoulders. One bullet could pierce my skin in a heartbeat.

We stand there for ten minutes, waving and smiling. I even give Roe an affectionate look and kiss Livingston. When Roe finally gestures for me to go back inside, I try not to appear to be struggling.

"That was excellent, Edelweiss," he applauds me. "If only you could be so well-behaved all the time."

"If only you could always be polite," I answer. "You're so amiable when you are, but then you spoil it by being horribly discourteous." Livingston kicks his father and shrieks something unintelligible. Roe sets him down without answering me.

"The poor boy doesn't have a chance at life," I lament.

"That's why we have to keep fighting. So that he does."

Nineteen

I toss and turn all night, being first hot, and then cold, but when I finally drift off, I sleep heavily. The full moon glares down at the still night. I shiver at how it casts its white shadow on my bed and the figure crouching beside me.

"Edelweiss," the man whispers. "Wake up, wake up." The wild look in his eyes echoes the panic in his voice. I shriek and bolt upright in bed.

"Shh," he hushes me, and as my eyes adjust to the darkness, I calm down. "We have to go to the basement. Quickly now."

I swing my legs out of bed, and he grasps my wrist, dragging me out of my room and into the hallway.

"Livingston," I murmur. "Where is he?"

King Roe doesn't respond.

"Livingston," I insist.

"Don't worry about him," he whispers in a hoarse voice as if his words were meant for a shout but suppressed into a whisper. "They won't hurt him."

I try to imagine what disturbance could awaken this midnight madness. We round a corner, and a dozen End Raider guards hurry in our direction.

"The rioters," one booms. "They're coming from the other side too."

"Rioters?" I ask Roe, fear clutching my voice.

"Yes," he answers.

My stomach muscles contract. King Roe bends down and pries a floorboard loose. I gasp as it reveals a hidden hatchway. He throws open the small door and retreats down a flight of stairs into a basement, beckoning me to follow. Cold blackness swallows us up as King Roe locks us in.

The dusty corner I sit in coats my palms with gray flakes. I clutch them to my knees and rest my chin on them. King Roe stands for a minute or so and then joins me. Before long, I begin to shiver, and my teeth chatter.

"If you want to tell me this is my fault, just say so," I mutter, sensing his silent fury.

"You are already aware, and I see no point in stressing the subject further," Roe replies coolly.

"Good." Half an hour goes by, and I'm exhausted but can't sleep in the cold, in the suspense, in the misery. Boredom soon enters the secret cellar. After what seems like several days and nights, but is only an hour, we hear footsteps from right above the hatchway.

"Where are the royals?" a man asks, stomping a foot simultaneously. It sounds like thunder from where I'm sitting, but my heart is pounding even louder. "The whole castle searched, and no royals."

"I'd even take the baby to rip apart," one growls. I gasp without thinking, and my husband springs a hand over my mouth.

"Oh no, we'd better move. I hear End Raiders on the way." I strain my ears and find that I can also detect a murmur coming from behind me.

"*Oh no, scary End Raiders,*" mocks a man with a feigned high-pitched voice. "*Whatever will we do, Pip?*"

"My name is Philip," the man corrects indignantly. "And we will run, obviously. They're coming right now."

"Ah, there's only two of 'em. We can take 'em out with the five of us."

"I don't know, Warren. They're mean lookin'."

"Brace yourselves. You too, Warren, Philip," a new voice interjects. The two End Raiders stomp over, and I can tell they are running because they come so quickly. The End Raiders and the castle rioters battle it out. My muscles tense when I hear the howls, gasps, and shrieks above me, merged with the crack of gunshots. If Roe wasn't holding my mouth so tight, I would be making several unintentional whimpers. Finally, the noises end, and there appears to only be one survivor of the scuffle.

"Pip?" the voice asks. I hear his knees boom against the ceiling. "Pip, come on, come on. Wake up now. Come on. Pip? Alright, you're Philip. Philip. Don't be sore at me. Pip! *Pip!*"

The faint howl of soft sobs comes from above me. I don't care that the man ridiculed the End Raiders. I don't care that he made nicknames his friend didn't like. I don't even care that he's trying to rip me apart. The sounds from the man are so pathetic that I want to run over and swing open the hatch. I want to comfort the man who has lost his friend.

When the rioter stands again, and his footfalls become distant, King Roe relinquishes his hold over my mouth.

"I feel for him," I remark. Roe shakes his head.

"There's no time for that. He doesn't want your sympathy. Pity yourself. Your home is being invaded by ruffians who want to kill you."

"Don't say that."

"It's the truth."

"It doesn't matter." I stand and begin to pace the room. "It feels better moving," I explain. When he doesn't reply, I continue. "But must it be so cold?"

"Did you expect a roaring fire waiting for you down here? This is an emergency escape for times like these."

"Yes, I realize, but surely it's not this cold outside."

"We're in a basement, do you not realize, child? It's colder underground. They tell me you are smart."

"Who's they?" I demand.

"My advisors."

"The same ones who instructed you to marry me?"

"What's it to you?"

"Never mind. But I've never been in a basement before."

"You mean your parents never had one?" the Raiders' king asks in disbelief.

"What's it to you?" I reply. If it weren't so dark, I would probably see him roll his eyes.

Pacing the room makes me feel warmer, but I soon become drowsy. I have to sit down after a couple of minutes, and before I know it, I'm unconscious on the basement floor.

"Wake up, child," King Roe shakes me. "It's safe now."

An End Raider official smiles. Light streams into the cellar.

"I hope that didn't disturb you too much," the official says to me. I stare at him and then at Roe.

"Don't worry," I tell him when Roe only shrugs. "It didn't faze me."

The next week follows just like it always has, but now, fear lingers with me more than anything. I don't mourn Ahmir's death as much as I have been, I stop raging at Roe for every little thing, and I'm not so lonely without the princesses. I am too anxious for all of that.

Every sound makes me jump. I stop and stare every time I pass the hallway with the loose floorboard, wondering if anyone could discover us in the future. I can't keep myself from peeking out the window periodically just to ensure another raid isn't occurring. I never go outside for fear that a rioter will snatch me off the doorstep and tear me into bits.

Even after a fortnight of nothing unusual, I don't relax. One day, I am eating dinner with Roe when we are served only water crackers and canned tomato soup.

"My queen," Roe begins.

"Yes?" I say while breaking a cracker in half.

"We're leaving."

I look up at him, my mouth slightly open.

"Oh no, sir, we can't."

"Why not?"

"Where will we go?"

"To the countryside."

I swallow and frown at my soup.

"Why?" I ask. The king laughs.

"For someone who cares so little about politics, you sure ask quite a few questions."

"This isn't politics. This is my life," I argue.

"Politics is your life, little girl."

I open my mouth to dispute, but I know it will do me no good.

"We leave in a week," he informs me.

I spend my last week in the castle packing my things. Everything I own has been bought for me since my arrival here, so I have no sentimental attachment to anything. As I dig through my last drawer, I empty out stockings and extra shoes until only a scrap of worn-down paper is left. I take the paper into my hands and unfold its creases. A smile plays on my lips as I gaze at the tear-stained paper. The black ink is hazy, and I can't read it, but I know exactly what it says.

My dearest Edelweiss-

Of all the things I am most sorry for, my deepest regret is letting you go. As you are already aware of, my father was forcing my hand in marriage. However, I want to tell you the truth about Lizzie Stoneman, or should I say Kinling. In fact, the girl isn't even related to the Stonemans, as her fake sister, Ms Eliza Stoneman, informed me. She has been arrested for her deceit and sentenced to a decade in prison. I never had any feelings for her, though it seems like an unjustly harsh punishment.

You are my one and only true love, so come back to me. My father has consented for me to marry you. Please, my dearest, accept my hand in marriage and stay with me forever. Return to the castle as soon as you receive this letter, and I will be there waiting.

Love always,

Ahmir

I stare down at the memorized letter from my dearest Everleigh. When I received it, I was the happiest girl on earth. Now, I am a woman, eighteen years old, and I find enjoyment impossible during most hours of the day.

Tomorrow, I leave for the countryside. King Roe assures me that everything will go as planned, and we will take a carriage to a villa where no rioters will wish to hurt us.

I grasp Prince Livingston in my arms, and again, fear takes over. With my late husband's love letter in my lap and my stepson pressed to my chest, panic rises in me. Livingston's three-year-old form squiggles in my grasp. His little feet push off against me.

"Alright, alright," I relent and let him out of my hold.

"Mama?" he asks timidly. His first word. I smile.

"Yes, Livingston?"

"Mama," he says again, his eyes shining. He has deep blue eyes, like his sisters, and not green eyes, like his father and brother, but they are just as beautiful.

Since I may be leaving this castle for good, I decide to explore the whole thing. It's so massive that I haven't investigated some of the hallways, but I resolve to do so now.

My shoes echo through a barren marble hall, and even when I try to step softly, they are noisy. I also fear getting lost, so I take them off as a marker.

Now everything is quiet, and I can slide my stockings along the smooth, cool floor. I turn each handle on one side of the hall, but they're all locked. I imagine I am in the maid's quarters, though it could also be office space or extra guest bedrooms. I press my ear to each door, wondering if anyone's in them, but they're all silent. I almost give up and turn back when I hear sounds from a door halfway down the hall.

I put my ear against the door crack and cup my ears around it. I know it's wrong to eavesdrop, but I can't help it. I realize that the muffled sound I hear is sobbing. Intrigued, I am even more curious about what room is on the other side of the door. I listen as a man whispers in a thick voice as one does when one cries. It's impossible to comprehend most of his words, but I understand a few.

"Why?" I hear over and over again. "I miss her. I'm sorry." The man apologizes to someone who doesn't reply. His heavy breathing wavers, and suddenly, I realize what a horrible thing I am doing.

Shame on me. I would be furious if someone listened to me have a meltdown. Quietly, I back away from the door and return down the hallway to retrieve my shoes.

For the rest of the day, I can't help but wonder whose room that is. I know it's dreadful that I am so prying, but I cannot turn my mind from it. I am contemplating this when Queen Lotus turns the corner.

"Lotus," I say, grateful to have her company.

"Heard you're leaving," she says. "I'm glad. There's no reason for you to stick around here."

"Aren't you going too?" I ask.

"No. I have lived here all my life. I'm not quitting on it yet."

"It's too dangerous," I say. "You could be killed."

"Girl, I've run that risk from the day I was born."

"How did you protect yourself from the rioters when they stormed the castle? You weren't in the cellar with Roe and I."

"I put on my overalls," she grins. "Blended right in."

"You amaze me," I tell her, gazing at her firm, wrinkled face.

"I may be an old woman, but I ain't incapable. I can take those rioters any day of the week."

"By the way, I ran into a hall I'm not familiar with. Do you know what rooms are there?"

"Lead the way," she says, and I show her to the marble corridor.

"These are the royal bedrooms," she tells me. "The founder of this palace lived in the first one down. The second one belonged to his son. Each heir after them had their own room, one after another. We're about halfway through now. Here's mine." Lotus points to the door directly before the one I eavesdropped on.

"So the next one down is your son's," I verify.

"Yes," she says. "Why do you ask?" I see no reason to hide the truth from her.

"I overheard someone in that room. He sounded... distressed. Was it Roe?"

Lotus smiles.

"The anniversary of his wife's death is today. My poor fellow lost her two years ago. He was telling me 'bout his regrets and boy, he sure has a lot of them."

"I'm sorry," I say. "I didn't mean to spy on you and him."

"Ah, don't fret. I'd never tell him." She winks at me and walks away. "Safe travels," she calls out over her shoulder. For the first time, I genuinely believe that Roe did not murder his wife, and a rush of compassion floods me. Perhaps we're not so different after all. Maybe in the country, my husband and I can become friends.

Twenty

I get into the carriage next to Roe and Livingston. The little one curls beside me, not old enough to realize our situation. Probably, he doesn't even know we are moving, and I envy him. I wish I didn't know as much as I do. The driver tosses my bags into the back of the carriage, and we lurch forward. I tap my foot to the rhythm of the horses' clip-clops and ignore my brooding husband.

After a few minutes, the castle gates open and we leave the grounds. Immediately, civilians surround us. Livingston squiggles in his seat to get a view of the people, but I grab his arm so he can't stand up. Most people staring at us are disgustedly shaking their heads, and I don't want Livingston to rile them by accident. King Roe is staring straight in front of him, so I do the same. We spend the next tense minutes like this, trying not to evoke bad feelings.

A shattering *crash* stops my heart, my head snapping to face the broken window. Shards of glass are spread across us, and Livingston shrieks. A rock thumps to the bottom of the carriage. Another comes hurtling again but only manages to dent the carriage exterior.

King Roe stops the driver and faces me.

"Come out of the carriage. Quickly now." He stumbles out and brushes glass from his purple robe, but I don't move. "Come on," he coaxes, lifting his son into his arms. A crowd hovers around, watching in silence. Still, I don't move, and when Roe lunges to grab my wrists, I tug them away.

"No," I whine.

"What do you mean, you stupid child? Come out immediately." I try to force myself to climb out, but something stops me. I have always had an impulse to run in times like this, but now I feel trapped by all these people.

"No," I insist. Rage is etched deeply in the lines of the king's face.

"Do you know what you're doing?" he whispers. I try to swallow, but I find it impossible. I probably don't know what I'm doing. Every time I make a decision, it seems to be the wrong one. I shift toward him in my seat and ease out of the vehicle. The snarling crowd breaks into savage chaos.

Everyone sprints at once. They pounce on the three of us, hitting, kicking, and shrieking. I scream as one man rips my pearl necklace from me and a woman grasps my hair. I am thrown to the ground, and my pink gown is covered in dust. I see shreds of the material clenched in fists, and even a child begins to beat up on me, which hurts more than anything else. Children are innocent things, and the hatred that burns in this one's eyes as he punches me is the worst kind of beast.

Livingston howls, though he is the safest from danger. Nobody hurts the little boy, no matter how violent they are. The ire is directed at his parents, and he sits alone, muddy tears mixed with dust streaking down his face. I am as helpless as he is, and the more I struggle, the worse it is for me. I can't get a view of Roe through the mass of bodies, but I imagine he is taking the same abuse as I am.

I hear a gunshot crack, and at first, I am afraid my husband is killed, but then I realize the bullet was shot upward. A uniformed man draws near as the mob backs away. When they step back, I see Roe lying on his side in the opposite direction, not moving.

"Step away, everyone. Come on, give them some air. I'm the sheriff." A badge gleams in the sunlight on his sheriff's uniform. He pulls the king to his feet, who groans and sways as if about to fall again. The sheriff attaches shackles to his wrists and guides him toward the police buggy.

"Get the queen," he calls over his shoulder. The sheriff is a brawny man with dark hair on his head, arms, and above his lip. He is lean and tall, with a sturdy posture. A couple deputies place me next to my husband in the prisoners' section of the buggy and hand me Livingston, still bawling. The sheriff waves away the mob without even punishing them for beating up the king and queen while the deputies close the backside of the buggy and lock us in.

I assess my own damage first. I'm sore all around, but the worst of my injuries is a swelling black eye, something painful in my ribs, and a large cut spewing blood out of my thigh. Not to mention all the bruises and scrapes I've acquired as well.

I examine Livingston in my lap and am relieved to see that his only mark is a cut on his shin from the smashed window. I can't say the same for my husband.

Roe is gulping in air and shuddering as if it hurts to do even that much. Blood seems to be leaking from all over him, and bruises disfigure his face. He turns to look at me with difficulty.

"Those people," he gasps. "Hate us."

I bite my lip.

"We've been arrested," I whisper. "What are they going to do to us? To Livingston?" The corners of Roe's mouth quiver, beads of red liquid forming.

"I already told you, child."

"And what was that?" He struggles to reply, his mouth slightly ajar, halfway to a smirk.

"They'll kill us."

Anger shoots through me.

"Why are you like this? Why have you given up on life?"

"I haven't, child. I've just given up on... blind optimism." His eyes seem to lose focus, and his muscles relax.

"Please don't leave me," I mutter, fear as acute as my anger has just been.

"You never needed me," he sighs, his eyelids blinking once.

"What about Maddie Jane and Maddie Grace?" I demand, frantic to change the conversation, as if not talking about death will keep him alive.

"They have each other."

"But having each other won't keep them from trouble."

Roe sighs, making a strange sound with his throat.

"Nothing will keep us from trouble now. If I don't die momentarily, I'll perish soon enough."

"No, don't say that. You don't mean it. Why do you say things you don't mean?"

"Why do you ask such dim-witted questions, little girl? Don't you know how draining it is?" I don't reply for fear of 'draining' him further. Livingston sobs in my arms, quieter now. The buggy stops, and the sheriff and his deputies bring us into the prison.

"What's the matter with the king?" one deputy asks. The sheriff doesn't answer immediately, taking time to look my husband up and down.

"The nurse will take care of him," he decides and drags Roe down a different hallway.

"This way, Your Majesty," the other deputy says when I am about to follow them. I nod and follow the men, listening to their conversation and holding my stepson.

"I don't see why Sheriff Campbell is taking Roe to the clinic. Heaven knows he'll be executed anyway."

Tears fill my eyes as I trail behind them. They speak as if I'm not even here.

"I'm not sure that's the clinic they're going to. I think they're doing it right now."

I gasp unintentionally. Both deputies turn to me.

"What is it? I thought you hated your husband. You said so in your speech." They chuckle darkly. My face flushes.

"I-" but I can't finish the sentence. I don't know why I care so strongly that Roe's not killed. After all, I *do* loathe him most of the time. The men laugh again, and we keep walking. "Any decent person should care if someone's going to be executed," I say finally.

"Says the one who detests all of humanity."

"Well, you're certainly not helping my opinion," I snap.

"I don't care about *your opinion*, puppet."

"I'm not a puppet; I'm your queen." I can't see their faces, but I can hear a smirk through their voices.

"Those are synonymous when it comes to you and the End Raiders." We don't say anything more because we arrive at the cell.

"There you go. Marlow will see you in the morning." They slam the cell door and leave me alone with Livingston. My eyes must adjust to the dim lighting that initially seems black but turns to a soft gray. Cold concrete surrounds me, and dust covers the wooden table in the center of the cell. On it is an empty tin cup and a damp bench beside it.

There's no window, but three unlit candles sit on a ledge. Two hammocks are attached to the walls, which I put Livingston in. A small cutout in the door can be opened from the outside to put food and drink through. I observe the dismal room and wonder if it will be my last home before death. Then I question if Roe will live to see it.

Eventually, I lay down with Livingston and try to sleep. The cell's air is frigid, though I attempt to share body heat with the baby.

"Woe," he whispers.

I smile sadly. Not many kids' second words are 'woe.'

"I know, Livingston. Your life really has begun with woe." Livingston frowns.

"Woe," he repeats.

"There's nothing I can do," I say. "I'm sorry."

There is a sharp knock at the door, and the sheriff drags in a bandaged Roe. Then I realize what Livingston means. Not woe; Roe.

"Edelweiss?" he asks, his voice and footsteps echoing in the small cell. "Are you in here too?"

"Yes, yes, I am," I shout, knowing I'm not alone anymore.

"Maybe you won't die after all."

"Why?" My spirits lift. If ever a pessimist such as Roe says something hopeful, I *know* something good has happened.

"Your fiance's here, and he will break you out."

I have to think about this for a second. I don't have a fiance, but then I realize his meaning.

"Marlow! The deputy said something about Marlow. Vashti Marlow!"

"Yes. The nurse got another patient in more dire need than I, so she had to leave. Vashti Marlow came in and explained to me that he works here."

"That's impossible," I interrupt. "Vashti runs a family business where I used to live."

"Not anymore. After your father was arrested, he moved here to work near him. I don't know why. Apparently, he's a very accommodating person." For some reason, he sounds sarcastic.

"He always has been, and this is the first time I'm grateful," I almost giggle.

"You better be because he's getting you out of quite the fix. He says he'll break you out with your father and Lizzie Kinling, the fake."

"No!" I cry. "I mean- Lizzie's fine, but my father?"

"Would you rather stay behind?"

"Of course not, but- why my father too? What has *he* ever done good? He's a murderer."

Roe shakes his head.

"He might as well break the whole prison out. It wouldn't make a difference- either way, he'll be executed if he's caught."

"He won't be. I can't believe we're not going to die!"

Roe drops his gaze to the rotten legs of the bench and sighs.

"I've only met Marlow today, but I can already tell he's crazy."

"Well, yes," I say. "He'd have to be to do this for us." Even as I say it, I finally recognize all the regard I've never had for Vashti. "If only I'd married him," I mutter more to myself than to Roe. "I wouldn't be here now."

"Yes, child," he agrees. "It was stupid to give him up, even for Ahmir."

Twenty-One

I shiver in my hammock, and no sleep follows. Everything seems desperate tonight. When morning finally comes, my hopes lift.

"The deputy said Vashti is coming this morning," I announce. "So we'll be saved. I'll convince him not to bring along my father." I watch Roe's face for joy, relief, or hope. His expression remains downcast.

"Good for you, Edelweiss," he says dryly.

"We're both in a better position than we were," I point out. "Surely you're happy."

Roe heaves a sigh that seems to stretch on for minutes. I scowl.

"You get on to me for moping. Look at yourself, you wet blanket."

"This blanket *is* wet," he agrees, clutching the blanket in his hammock.

"Hypocrite," I accuse him, though I'm unsure why I want to aggravate him.

"You're a strange thing," Roe remarks in a faint voice as if he's more muttering to himself than anything. "You were a princess dowager, and you were despondent. Then you were a queen, and you were still depressed. Now you're in prison, preparing for execution, and you've become an optimist." He sighs again bitterly.

"There wasn't any hope then. There's hope now."

"You mean because your ex-fiance is here, and he appears to have forgiven you for running away with another man."

"He never wanted to marry me. He was probably happy when I left."

My husband breaks into a fit of laughter, enraging me.

"Didn't want to marry you? I knew you were a fool, but such an idiot?"

"It was forced upon us. Our parents arranged our marriage. It's not like he proposed or something." I am instinctively defensive but without reason. So what if he does want to marry me? All the better for him.

"Answer me this, child. Why would he move away from his family, work where your father's imprisoned, offer to sacrifice his life for your escape, and *not* want to marry you?"

"Because he has a big heart," I reply, but I don't believe myself.

"Big heart? People don't do things because they have a big heart. They do it to benefit themselves."

"How is breaking us out going to benefit him?"

"Don't you understand? He's not going to help me, no matter what he says. Do you think it will just be you, me, and him? No. It'll be him and you. He would kill me in an instant if I stood in his way. *You're* what's in it for him."

"You speak nonsense," I shout, and though he stops talking, he chuckles.

"Besides," I continue. "He's bringing along Lizzie and my-"

A knock on the door interrupts me.

"Marlow?" Roe calls out.

"Yes," replies a voice I never thought I'd hear again. It brings me back to the times before I met Ahmir. He puts a key into the lock and opens the door. His face looks almost the same, though he has a beard now, and his hair is cut shorter.

"Vashti!" I shriek. Vashti turns to me, but he doesn't smile back. He shakes his head and strides toward my husband, carrying a goblet.

"Good morning, Miss Chapel."

"I'm not a Chapel anymore," I reply fiercely, though my stomach drops at his cold reply.

"Oh yes, Queen Edelweiss," he corrects himself without so much as a flicker of a smile. "Long time no see."

"Vashti, I-" but I don't know what to say. Sorry for leaving you? Please help me? A million possibilities come to me. He puts a hand up.

"No, no," he says. "Nothing more. I have come on duty. This is a goblet of wine for the king." Roe's eyes move from the goblet to the man's face, back down again.

"Poison?" he whispers. Vashti nods almost undetectably. My eyes widen.

"No," I warn. "Don't drink it."

Roe turns to face me.

"I have no choice. Marlow is offering me the luxury way to die."

"But can't you just escape? Vashti, isn't he escaping with us?" Vashti gives me a stern look.

"I changed my mind."

Roe snorts.

"What did I tell you?"

I stare helplessly at Vashti.

"I can't go without my husband."

"Edelweiss, they want his blood," Vashti argues. "If he breaks out with us, we'll be caught and killed. Right now, they're plotting the most painful death for him they can muster. They'll torture him if we're caught. The safest thing for this man is to be poisoned, and he knows it."

"Your fiance is right, little girl. And on the plus side, once I'm out of the way, you're free to marry again."

Vashti turns slightly red.

"I don't *want* to marry again," I spit back at Roe. "I already hate my devotion to you."

"I would hardly call it devotion, but the thought's nice."

"Edelweiss, please," Vashti implores. "Spare your husband from a terrible death and let him exit quickly. He'll be dead within an hour. I'll notify every one of his death, and in the confusion, we'll slip out quietly. No one will even notice."

"I don't care if no one notices. I just don't want him to die."

"Who are you, and what have you done with my wife?" Roe scoffs. "You're supposed to hate me."

"Fine," I snap. "If you want to drink the poison, be my guest. I was only trying to spare your miserable life."

Roe holds the goblet in his hand and looks me in the eye.

"When you escape, take Livingston with you. I want the Raiders to live on."

"Of course I will, but is that what you care about? The End Raiders? How about your son's life?"

"Yes, that too. And if you can, keep my daughters from harm."

"You don't care about them. You're the one who cast them away," I accuse.

"I didn't cast them away, you half-baked little girl. I was saving them. I knew we'd be in trouble after your famous little speech at Ahmir's funeral. I didn't want them to suffer, too." Tears come to my eyes. I have always thought Roe sent them to boarding school as an act of revenge against me, not for a noble reason.

"Thank you. I'm glad you did."

"Of course you are, though you whined about it enough."

"I don't mean to rush you," interrupts Vashti. "But we really need you to drink that so we can alert the authorities in an hour. Then we'll leave."

Roe nods.

"Goodnight, Edelweiss."

"But it's only morning," I cry. "Don't go yet. Please? I need you to stay with me." Roe gives me a tight smile and leans back the goblet.

"No!" I shriek. "Stop it! Vashti, tell him to stop. Don't die. Please!" I lunge forward to knock the cup from his hand, but Vashti grabs me.

"Let him go, Edelweiss." I fall to my knees and sob, though it's hard to know why. It's like Ahmir dying all over again. Hope, yet again, sucked out of me, although this time, it's an allusion. Hope is still there, for me, at least.

The hour passes slowly, and once the goblet is drained, Roe lies on his hammock and closes his eyes. I run to him and grasp his arm, pleading, yelling, howling for him to stay alive. He sighs several times but ignores my calls. I put my hands around his swollen face, and for the first time, I kiss my second husband. Long and hard, I press my lips to his, and I yearn to suck the toxin from his body.

I don't know when Vashti leaves, but when I finally look up, he's gone. My husband doesn't move.

"Roe? Roe, please. If you're alive, then answer me, please. Please!" I shriek. I watch his lips part.

"Endure, my child,
through horrid days.
Wicked and wild
are the Realm's ways."

I remember how he cherishes poetry, so I recite a poem from deep in my heart. It is one that I have desperately tried to remember but have found impossible until now.

"When finally the cold skies were clear,
I was looking all over for my dear
Everleigh.

I searched in all her favorite places,
But alas, I couldn't find any traces
Of Everleigh.

I thought of somewhere else to be,
Straining my eyes around to see
Everleigh.

Under the ice's shivery hold,
I found her body lying ice cold,
Dear Everleigh.

When she froze, her eyes did gloss,
How will I bear the terrible loss
Without Everleigh?"

Roe gives a half smile, his eyes still closed. "That's the poem you wanted when Ahmir died."

"Yes," I breathe. "I didn't know I remembered it."

"Poetry awakens in a reader when it remembers the emotion its writer had when he first wrote it."

"Is that true?" I ask in wonder. Roe struggles to answer, the poison beginning to affect him.

"I've always believed it to be. Do you know the name of that poem?"

"No, but I imagine it's called Everleigh."

"It's not," he replies.

"But you told me you had never heard it before."

Roe grimaces before responding.

"My head feels funny. And yes, I lied. It's titled 'Drowning.' I should know. I wrote it."

"Who is Everleigh?" I ask, rubbing tears off my face. I don't care that the dying man deceived me. It doesn't matter anymore.

"She was my wife, the one everyone says I murdered." I shudder to think if anyone accused me of killing Ahmir.

"Did you?" I ask.

"No. It happened exactly as the poem says. She drowned. Oh, I can feel it happening."

"What? What is happening?"

"I'm dying, in case you've forgotten."

"Tell me something," I say through my tears. "Ahmir didn't get to choose his last words. You do."

"Here's something," he mutters with difficulty. "I always wondered how such a flawed... broken... impure girl could be named after a flower. Now I realize. It's not in your nature to be who you're expected to be. You are always the opposite but somehow just as good.... I didn't marry you for political reasons. I just wanted you to be Everleigh. You weren't, and I don't love you any less."

My tears keep coming, but they are quiet now. I kneel by my husband's hammock and grasp his hand until it goes limp in mine, and he exhales for a final time.

I used to think that his only pleasing feature is his eye color, but now they're closed, and his face bloats with cuts and bruises. Yet somehow, he is the most beautiful corpse in the world, and when I kiss him again, it's not a frantic way of keeping him alive but a gesture of surrender to my husband, to my grief, to the End Raiders, and to my own hatred.

"When Ahmir died, I figured the love in my life was gone. I was wrong then. Maybe I am now."

Even if he doesn't hear my last words to him, *I* do, and I need those words more than he does.

Twenty-Two

"The king! The king is dead," Vashti yells, sprinting down the jail hall. I sit in my hammock, my eyes shut tight. I don't dare open them for fear of catching a glimpse of the body sprawled out in his hammock.

As the news spreads, I hear gasps, voices, and footfalls. Everyone tries to understand exactly what has occurred, and I know they will all parade into my cell to find out. Vashti leads the pack inside: the sheriff, deputies, soldiers, and nurse rush through the doors. Vashti makes a slight motion with his head toward me.

"Alright," he announces. "I'll take the queen to another cell for now." The sheriff nods his approval, preoccupied with the dead king. I pick up Livingston and fight through the crowd until I reach Vashti. "Let's go," he whispers, and we leave the chaos, though we don't go far until we reach another cell.

"Your father and Lizzie Kinling are in here," he warns me before opening the door.

"Let's not take my father," I reply, reminding him of my preference. Vashti shakes his head.

"No, better take him too. Once they discover the jailbreak, they'll torture him for answers. Even if we must abandon him later, taking him now is only decent." I get a fluttering feeling in my stomach when I wonder how my father will react to seeing me again. Vashti finds the right key and turns the handle, swinging the door open.

The room is dimly lit by candles, so I have to squint to see the two figures huddled in the corner. One hammock is hung precisely like the two in my cell, but the second one is around the two figures' shoulders, serving as a blanket. The people look up at us, and all I can make out are two dirt-covered faces staring back at me with wide eyes full of hunger.

"Ed?" a scratchy voice calls. Though he sounds hoarse and weak, I recognize the tones of my father.

"Edelweiss, Vashti," a young woman cries, also familiar. Vashti walks to them and offers both of his hands. They each take one and stand up with difficulty. Their bodies are thin, and they look famished. My father's face is unshaven, and Lizzie Kinling's blond hair is tangled and matted. They stumble toward me.

I can't look my father in the eye, but I embrace Lizzie. I'm gentle, though she trembles in my hold and grasps me with an iron grip. She begins to sob and doesn't let go of my neck, though her arms and shoulders shake.

"Thank you," she weeps. "Don't leave me here. Don't leave me, please." I try to pry her from me, but she's unmovable.

"Lizzie," Vashti says. "We have to go. We don't have time to stand around."

"I'm sorry, yes," she responds, withdrawing from me. We hurry down the hall, my father and I not acknowledging each other. Vashti leads us out of the jail, carrying Livingston, and we all start to sprint. I'm not sure how far we go, but even with Lizzie's frailness, it must be a mile before we slow to a walk and converse.

Vashti leads the discussion. "We need to find a way to leave Seth Sound. We should go to Chan Hinge. Surely, they'll take in the queen of the End Raiders."

"No," I reject quickly, remembering my stay there during my honeymoon. "No, they wouldn't leave us alone. They'll listen to us if we give them money and gifts, but we can't do that. We don't want to lead the End Raiders. If we don't give them what they want, they'll probably kill us, just like here."

"Then we need to go to Cap," suggests my father.

"No," I repeat. "They're almost as bad as Seth Sound, and as soon as word spreads that the king is dead, they'll turn on us as well."

"Then where can we go?" Lizzie wonders.

"Nowhere," I respond. "Nowhere is safe if people recognize me or my father."

"We can go home, where we all used to live," Lizzie says. "I want to see my family again."

"What about the Chapels? They'll be recognized," Vashti points out.

"No one will care if *I* go back. I offended no one but the king. Let's go home, Vashti. You and I have family there. We can't shape our whole lives around the Chapels."

"Are you abandoning me?" my father demands.

"I won't leave them," Vashti says quickly. "You can go home, Lizzie. We'll go with you, but then Edelweiss and I will leave." I am alarmed by his distinction of 'he and I.' I decide to make my intentions clear.

"I've been widowed twice, Vashti. I'll never remarry.".

"You'll think differently later," Vashti tries to assure me. "We won't jump into anything just yet." I shake my head but don't pursue the subject further. I'm not the only one who's changed since we last saw each other.

"Well, maybe people will forgive me for my crime now that everyone's against the End Raiders," my father says.

"It's too risky," Vashti tells him. "Our village has always been Raider-loving, and even with a divided kingdom, I know which side our neighbors are on."

Livingston begins to kick Vashti and press his hands against his chest in an attempt to be put down. Vashti does, and we all sit, exhausted from our travels.

"We've been moving for a while," Vashti says. "We've got to be close to the city's edge, and from there, we'll be better off."

"Can we hitchhike?" I ask.

"Certainly not," my father replies. He doesn't have to explain. We all know some people would be willing to take us in, but too many citizens will bring us right back to prison, if not worse.

We go a little farther tonight, but eventually, we have to stop. We're invited to sleep in a nice clump of bushes off the road, and though it's uncomfortable, it works. I remember the last time I slept in nature. That was when I ran away from home, and the dowager queen Lotus saved me. The thought stops my heart from pumping. I sit straight up.

"Lotus!" I gasp aloud. Everyone looks at me.

"What about her?" Lizzie asks.

"She wasn't taken. She's probably still at the castle." Everyone glances at me and then at each other.

"Well, yes, I suppose so," Vashti says.

"She must be looking for us," I explain. "She *must*." I'm unsure if this is true, but it seems to be our only hope.

"I don't know, Ed," my father mutters. "She doesn't even know we escaped, and if she does get the news, she's as likely to find us as everyone else is."

"She knows where I live," I say after considering his words. "Remember when I ran away, Father?" I address him for the first time since the incident.

"I remember," he says. "That's the last time we saw each other."

"Yes, and I slept in the berry patch. Lotus found me there and brought me to the train station. That's where we need to go. We don't have to get out of the city. She'll eventually find us if we wait there. That's the only place to start." Everyone grins in appreciation.

"There's a platform five miles away," Lizzie tells us. "We can walk there in the morning."

"None of us has any money," I say. "But I'm sure Lotus has stacks. We can buy our way to freedom." We all lay back down again. Sleeping with a plan fixed in our minds is much easier.

The following day, we do as we said and walk five miles to the train station. My father and I find an outhouse in which we hide. The others watch for Lotus from the corner of the train station.

"So, Eddy," my father says. "It's been a long time since I've seen you."

"Oh yeah," I reply sarcastically. "The last time you shot my husband."

"I know I can't ask you to put that behind us."

"No, you can't."

"I'm sorry, if it means anything to you."

"It doesn't."

My father is silent.

"I never meant to hurt *you*. But why did you have to marry the only two men I despise?"

"Because I loved one of them and learned to love the other."

"Maybe that makes me a bad father. You love the people I hate. But perhaps it's the other way around."

"You think I'm a bad daughter? You're the murderer."

"As if you haven't done anything wrong out of grief, Ed. Your mother had just died. I lost my only daughter. You, of all people, should understand what that's like."

"I do, Father, I really do, but I made a terrible speech, and you killed the prince."

"But your speech led to the king's death," my father argues. I am silent. "I'm sorry, Ed, if you hate me for what I did, but you can't blame me for having hated you."

I don't answer.

Twenty-Three

"It's her!" Lizzie cries. "Edelweiss, Mr Chapel, it's her!"

Nearly twenty-four hours since being cooped up with my father in a dark, cramped outhouse, I hear Lizzie hollering.

We burst out of our hiding place, completely disregarding how dangerous this is. I run to the overalled farmer who is holding the hands of two identical-looking girls.

"Maddie Jane! Maddie Grace!" I call, and the two girls jump on me.

"I missed you!" Maddie Grace shrieks.

"Don't ever leave again," Maddie Jane orders.

"We have to go," my father says, his head down so no one will recognize him. I nod.

"Let's go east," Vashti decides, and we follow him out of public sight. Lotus is the first to speak.

"I knew I'd find you here at one of these stations. When you and Roe were arrested, I visited my granddaughters' school. There, I learned of your escape, so I took them out. You were easy to find since I knew which slammer you fled from."

"We wouldn't have been able to escape if it wasn't for Vashti," I reply. Vashti gives me an appreciative glance.

"You're the reason I started working at the jail," he replies. Lizzie frowns.

"You said it was for me," she pouts. "Now it's for Edelweiss?" Vashti's cheeks glow pink.

"Well, it was for both of you, really," he stammers sheepishly. Lotus chuckles.

"I love boys," she says, elbowing me. I'm uncertain what she means, and I can't say I agree.

"Anyway," Vashti continues, switching discussions. "What are we going to do from here?" We are all silent for a minute.

"I brought a lot of money," Lotus offers. "We could buy a couple villas in the country." We all nod our agreement.

"Yes, and Vashti will buy them because nobody will recognize him," my father adds.

"Do we have enough money to last us a lifetime?" Lizzie inquires.

"We might if we only buy a small cottage and are conscious of what we spend," Lotus replies. "Even then, there's eight of us, including Livingston, so we'll have to work." Lizzie bites her lip.

"I'm used to lavish living," she admits. "We Kinlings have always been rich. And besides, will we ever be able to meet other people without worrying about being caught?"

"I'm okay," Vashti says. "And the little ones should be alright, too. I doubt Lotus will be recognized in her farmer outfit. However, Lizzie, Edelweiss, and Mr Chapel will have to be careful." I swallow, thinking about a life in hiding. I suppose it will be alright in the country, married to Vashti and on a tight budget. Just like I always knew I would be.

My life seems to be going in a circle. I feel as if I have run a long race as a princess, completing a lap, then as queen, sprinting a lap more. Now I'm back where I started, still poor, still engaged to Vashti, still hopeless of a better life, but now I am breathless and tired from what I have endured already.

We are quiet for a minute but then suddenly stop. Three men stride up to us, brows knitted into scowls and teeth yellow and jagged. We stand together, holding our breath and staring down at the ground

"Hey Marty," one man addresses his tall companion. "Don't some of 'em folk look familiar?" They gaze at us.

"They do, don't they? That young lady, especially."

"And the guy with the scar on his cheek," a paunchy man with a bushy mustache pipes up, pointing to my father.

"Weren't they in the newspaper?" the tall man named Marty queries. I squeeze my eyes shut, preparing for the worst. Nobody in my little party moves.

"In the politics section," the portly man adds.

"Is that the queen?" Marty gasps. The man who talked first, with sallow skin and a prominent nose, looks shocked.

"It sure is," he answers.

"Well, I'll be," the short man mutters.

"What do we do, Dan?" Marty asks. I watch Vashti's shoes begin to move again, and soon, we all turn around and walk quickly in the opposite direction. The men's voices, however, only seem to get closer as they follow us.

"Let's take 'em in," Dan tells his comrades. "If we turn them in, we'll get the reward money." There's a doubtful pause.

"We can't take all of 'em," Harvey points out. "There's too many." We speed up our paces, but the three men following us are just as quick.

"Then let's grab the three fugitives and be done with it," Marty replies. The discussion seems to end and I hear a small shriek as Harvey puts a hand on Lizzie's shoulder.

"Please!" she cries. "Please go away. I can't take it." The men make no response, each taking hold of an escapee. Dan's hand is huge and muscular around my arm. I cringe and attempt to tug away, but he doesn't let go.

The whole group of us begins to plead, our voices trying to drown out the ruthless growls of the men.

"We're only poor folk."

"We didn't do wrong, we didn't!"

"Let us go. Please let us go."

"Have pity on us."

"We'll pay you anything."

"We're already going to get a reward for you," Dan replies. "And we only want the criminals." Our voices progressively get more desperate, but Harvey, Marty, and Dan get increasingly stubborn. Finally, Vashti resorts to combat, swinging the first punch.

He aims at Marty's nose but hits his forehead instead. After that initial blow, everything becomes confused, and punches are thrown around between my father, Vashti, Dan, Marty, and Harvey. I take Livingston in my arms and push the princesses out of the fight as we run. Lizzie follows, though she is slower, and my mother-in-law takes up the rear.

We run like we did escaping the jail, except not as far. We dash back into town, where we find many men with guns lined up. Lizzie whimpers, and the little girls cling to me, breathless. Only Lotus keeps her senses and approaches the men in her farmer disguise.

"What are you all doing?" she asks the group.

"Man hunting," they reply, showing their rifles to her. "There are prisoners on the loose. Three of them. We're going to get them and-" An astonished cry interrupts the man speaking.

"Claude! Is that the two little ladies we're looking for?" Everyone yells their agreement, and there's a minor tussle before they approach Lizzie and me. Then, I see more familiar faces from my past. Two men from my old life stand side by side, signaling to us.

John Kinling, or as he is always referred to as, John K, stands next to the banker, Mr Greene. John K rushes over to his daughter, laughing and pulling her into a buggy wagon where Mr Greene sits, ready to make an escape.

"Edelweiss!" he calls out to me as several men run to us, firing their guns. The last time I saw Mr Greene was when Ahmir died, and now I dive into his buggy as he's about to take off. I position Livingston into Lizzie's arms and help Maddie Jane and Maddie Grace up. John K grasps a rifle and sits in the back of the buggy with us while Mr Greene commands the horses to go. The manhunters begin shooting wildly, but we duck, and they only accomplish spooking the horses. They leap and gallop us away at full speed.

"What about Vashti?" Lizzie asks me. "We have to go back for him." I bite my lip and frown. If we return for Vashti and my father, we might not get away in time, but they will never otherwise escape. Mr Greene shouts us the same question from the front of the buggy.

"Where's your father, Edelweiss?" Lizzie and Lotus stare at me for an answer. I close my eyes and think about all the anger I've stored away for my father. He has been making my life miserable for too long. He abandoned my mother and me, leaving us poor. He cares more for politics than he does for his own family. He sold me to Vashti, even though I never wanted him.

And Vashti. Vashti will die if I don't go back for him. The looming threat of my marriage to him hangs over my head. *Although,* a small voice reminds me, *he did rescue me from prison.* If we don't go back for them, will I regret it? I have to answer Mr Greene right now because the opportunity will be passed if I wait any longer.

"They're dead," I say finally. "They were killed on our way here." Lizzie turns her gaze to her feet and swallows.

"I'm sorry, Edelweiss," Mr Greene expresses.

"Then Vashti will never know how I love him," Lizzie whispers, barely audible.

The drive is long and miserable. It rains at one point, and I catch Lizzie silently weeping. John K doesn't speak to anyone but his daughter, though I'm not surprised. He was always arrogant when I lived in the village and never kind or considerate.

Lotus begins to cough and develops a cold. The two little girls are restless and agitated, undoubtedly missing their parents. They are parentless now and have seen much tragedy in their lives, including the death of their brother. I can't stop thinking that I, too, am most likely an orphan by now.

After several days of buggy riding, we finally arrive at our destination: a massive mansion with expansive windows letting in the sun. A dense forest surrounds it on all sides, and there is barely a pathway, let alone a road, that leads to it.

"It's a secret family home," John K explains. "It has been in the Kinling family for centuries, passed down through generations. My father first brought me here when I was twelve. Even you, Lizzie, haven't been here before." Lizzie looks at the house in wonder, but then her expression turns to sorrow.

"Father," she begins. "Will we live here forever?" John K sighs and shrugs.

"Yes, my dear girl, but don't look so sad. Your mother and brother are here, and now you have new friends," he tells her, gesturing to Lotus, Maddie Jane, Maddie Grace, Livingston, Mr Greene, and myself. "The ten of us will live together. There's plenty of space."

"I'll never have another party," she reflects wistfully. Just as she says this, her family runs out of the house. Snobbish Mrs Kinling and mischievous Thomas come to reunite with their family.

"Martha! Thomas!" laughs John K. I step aside as the family hugs. I brush away a tear and hear Lotus cough beside me.

"Ah Edelweiss," she says. "Don't worry about having kinfolk around. You have us, now."

"I want to be happy for them," I tell her. "But their family is unbroken, and I'm an orphan. How do they expect me not to be jealous?"

"Think of me. I've lost my husband, my son, my daughter-in-law, my grandson, both my parents, *and* my older sister. You get used to it." I can't imagine that I ever will, though. Not entirely.

Twenty-Four

Three Years Later

Sometimes, I wake up in the morning feeling miserable, and regret fills my body. When this happens, I remind myself how well things worked out.

I am raising Livingston, now a handsome six-year-old. His sisters are fifteen. Maddie Jane loves to sew and makes us all new clothes. Maddie Grace is the family's gardener; we all get fresh vegetables because of her.

I turn twenty-one today, and my best friend, Lizzie, is baking me a cake. Mr Greene and John K are in town, but Lizzie and I can't go for fear of being recognized.

The authorities haven't found us yet. Mr Greene discovered that most people believe Lizzie, Lotus, the royal kids, and I to be dead, as we have vanished, although they are only right about Lotus. She died in her old age a little over a year ago.

But what I am most grateful for is the fact that I have found a way to compensate for my grief. I am a poet now, taking a leaf from my second husband's book. I write my poems in a journal, which is now filled with verses and rhymes I am proud of. Poetry has soothed the wildness I have within me. I release into my work all the hatred, anger, regret, guilt, and sadness I have, just as Roe used to do.

I allow Lizzie to read my poems, and she is constantly amazed by them. Lizzie has yet to get her life back. Her joy came from society, and that has been stripped from her. However, we are optimistic that she will soon find a new hobby to occupy herself with.

Mrs Kinling couldn't bear the life thrown at her, so she and Tommy moved out within a month of living there. She is still part of the family, however, as she provides us with half the casino's earnings. Mr Greene still owns the bank, and John K is the local school's superintendent. They pretend they never saw Lizzie and me again, and everyone believes them.

Livingston will never get a chance at a normal childhood, but I hope he can one day live among everyone else without fear of being in trouble. He and his sisters are pleased with their lives. They rely on each other for company and enjoy the beauty of nature.

The question of whether or not we should have gone back for my father and Vashti haunts me. I try to tell myself that it's in the past, but the decision still feels fresh even three years later. They didn't make it to their happy endings. Vashti was shot, and my father died in prison.

The End Raiders have collapsed, and the kingdoms are separate again, though I can't be sure this is the last the Realm will hear of the empire. *Until the end,* they proclaim, but how will they know when The End has come? Perhaps it has arrived already, or maybe their saga has only begun.